An Elegy for Easterly

PETINA GAPPAH

ff

faber and faber

ᵔ

First published in 2009
by Faber and Faber Ltd
Bloomsbury House, 74–77 Great Russsell Street
London WC1B 3DA
This paperback edition first published in 2010

Typeset by Faber and Faber Ltd
Printed in England by CPI Bookmarque, Croydon

The poem 'Optimism' by Jane Hirshfield on p. ix is taken from her volume *Each Happiness Ringed by Lions* (2005) and appears courtesy of Bloodaxe Books

The lyric by Oliver Mtukudzi on p. 239 is from his song 'Ndima Ndapedza' (1998) and appears courtesy of Tuku Music

A CIP record for this book
is available from the British Library

ISBN 978–0–571–24694–6

2 4 6 8 10 9 7 5 3 1

For Tererai and Simbiso Gappah,
my beloved parents,
and for Regina, Ratiel, Vimbai and Vuchirai

❧ Contents ❧

More and more I have come to admire resilience.
Not the simple resistance of a pillow, whose foam
returns over and over to the same shape, but the
    sinuous
tenacity of a tree: finding the light newly blocked
    on one side,
it turns in another. A blind intelligence, true.
But out of such persistence arose turtles, rivers,
mitochondria, figs – all this resinous, unretractable
    earth.

                        Jane Hirshfield, 'Optimism'

❦ At the Sound of the Last Post ❦

The bugle call shatters the stillness of the shrine. Its familiar but haunting melancholy cannot fail to move. Even the President seems misty-eyed behind his glasses. Close to him in the widow's place of honour, I am aware of his every movement. I watch him without moving my eyes. Perhaps it is not mist in his eyes but the film of my own sudden tears. The badges sprinkled on his sash of office shimmer and recede against the green of the material.

He brings his hands together in a clasp that puts the sinews of both hands into relief. It makes him, for a fleeting moment, the very old man that he is. Unexpected pity wells up inside me. Half-remembered lines of poetry come unbidden to my mind: he grows old, he grows old; he shall wear the bottoms of his trousers rolled. There is a parting in his hair, where the white roots at his scalp show in the places that the dye has not reached. Does he count the years and maybe

3

just months and days that remain until he, too, is sounded away by that bugle to lie beneath the blackness of polished marble in the empty space next to the grave of his first wife?

The faces of the pallbearers are half-hidden by their olive berets. The sun glints on the metal insignias on their epaulettes. Their sabres are reflected on the polished surface of their shoes. They lift the coffin and hoist it upon their shoulders. The flag that covers the coffin slides on the smoothness to reveal the casket of white and gold. The soldiers in the front move their hands simultaneously to keep the flag from slipping away.

They march in a one-step pause two-step pause progression until they reach the grave that is lined in green felt. The white man from the funeral home is stiff in his top hat and tails. Where do they find them, these white men with their pinched faces above their funereal clothing?

There are almost no whites in the country now.

Everything is black and green and brown and white. Black is the marble of the polished gravestones and the mourning clothes. Green is the presidential sash and the olive colours of the berets on the heads of the soldiers and the artificial shining verdancy of the grave. Black is the dark of the gathered masses who listen to the youth choir dressed for battle in bottle-green fatigues, voices hoarse in the August heat, singing songs from a war that they are not allowed to forget. Black and brown are the surrounding Warren Hills, the hills denuded, with stumps remaining where the trees were, the green trees now the brown wood that replaces the electricity that is not to be found in the homes.

The bugle is still as the coffin is lowered. The sudden silence unsettles me out of my thoughts of presidential mortality. I get ready to move forward to walk down to the grave. The President moves also, and I watch him, an old man still, but one who is Commander of the Armed Forces, Defier of Imperialism, and, as he was just moments ago, Orator at the Funerals of Dead Heroes.

∾

Just under an hour ago, after the opening prayers and before the final salute, he gave his funeral oration.

'He was a fine man, a gallant soldier in the fight for our liberation, a loving husband and father. We condole with his family and his widow, Esther, and urge her to be brave at this time of inconsolable loss.'

The cameras of the national broadcaster found my face. I was beamed into televisions in homes across the country, brave in my inconsolable loss. The cameras moved back to the President as he said, 'I say to

5

you today that, much like the gallant hero we bury here today, you too must guard against complacency. You must follow the example of our fallen comrade who lies here. We must move forward today and strive ahead in togetherness, in harmony, in unity and in solidarity to consolidate the gains of our liberation struggle.'

I could see around me eyes glazing over at this seventh oration at the seventh hero's funeral in four months. They are being culled, all of them, age and Aids will do its work even among the most gallant of heroes; the Vice-President with the hooded eyes looks like he may be next to go. It must be easy pickings to be the President's speechwriter; all he seems to do to write a new speech is strike out the name of the previously fallen comrade and replace it with that of the newly dead.

The President spoke on. The Chief Justice nodded off. The Police Commissioner jerked to wakefulness as applause broke out. Only the Governor of the Central Bank seemed to listen, face strained with avid attention. At the funeral of the third dead comrade of the year, just a week after the Cabinet had finally agreed on the most patriotic figure at which the national currency should be exchanged against the pound and the euro and the dollar and the rand, the President had announced a different, even more patriotic figure.

I listened to the rhythm of his speech. Having addressed theme number one, the liberation struggle, it was time for the second theme. By the time I counted down from ten, he would have begun to attack the opposition.

As I reached *six*, his voice echoed out over the hills.

'Beware the puppets in the so-called opposition that are controlled from Downing Street. They seek only to mislead with their talk of democracy.'

The microphone hissed slightly at *puppets*, making it sound like *puppies*.

Downing Street was his cue to move to the next theme, the small matter of the country's sovereignty: 'I say to Blair and to Bush that this country will never, a trillion trillion times never, be a colony again.'

The microphone gave a piercing protest at the *trillion trillion*, making the phrase jump out louder than the other words. There was a nugget of newness in the use of *trillion* and not *million* as a measure of the impossibility of re-colonisation. It is three months since inflation reached three million three hundred and twenty-five per cent per annum, making billionaires of everyone, even maids and gardeners.

❧

The coffin has been lowered.

Rwauya, the eldest son of my husband, guides me

7

down to cast gravel into the grave. He has abandoned his usual dress of trousers of an indeterminate colour and shirts which usually manage to exhibit both the lurid colours of the national flag and the President's face. Still, the raw smell of unwashed Rwauya seeps through his crumpled suit. I try not to flinch as he takes my elbow and we follow the President past the graves of the men and two women who are buried here. My handful of dirt makes a splattered brown on the white surface of the coffin.

The family follows behind us. My husband's sister Edna breaks into loud keening. 'Brother,' she wails as she kneels beside the grave. 'Come back, my brother. Come back. You have not completed your tasks, brother. See how the nation longs for your return.'

She makes as though to jump into the grave, and is stopped by her daughters. She stumbles into the President's wife, the Second First Lady, who soothes her with a perfumed hand to the shoulder. As Edna heaves dry sobs against the black silk of the Second First Lady's suit, my eyes travel down to Edna's shoes. She really should start investing more money in her shoes; her unshaped peasant's feet require something stronger than cheap *zhing-zhong* plastic leather shoes to contain them.

That Edna makes a spectacle of herself is not surprising. She is given to bursts of emotion calibrated for public consumption. She is always ready to be offended on behalf of others. When I told their family twenty-one years ago that I was leaving her brother, she spoke to her sister in a whisper of theatrical resonance, the better to reach my ears.

'*Ngazviende*,' she said, 'and good riddance. Real women were divorced to make place for a *mhanje* such as this one.'

Thus my introduction to the word *mhanje*: their word for the lowest form of womanhood, womanhood without womanliness, *mhanje* being a barren woman, a woman without issue, unproductive, a fruitless husk. There was no question that it could be her brother who was infertile. He had proved his virility in the three children that he had with a woman he had been married to even as he was marrying me in London in a council office with no central heating before an official with mucus drip-dripping into his handkerchief.

I thought I loved him; but that was in another country.

I exulted to hear him say, 'I want a wife who shares in my dreams; an equal, not a subordinate.' I helped him to write furious letters of righteous indignation condemning the white-settler regime and the situation in his country. I forgot about the fight against apartheid in my own country as his battle seemed

9

more urgent. We wrote letters and hosted exiles and through long nights we argued about Fanon and Biko and Marx and Engels. That was before we arrived in the country after independence. Before I found out that my husband already had a wife with three children, whose names were not gentle on the tongue.

∾

Edna's grave-diving attempts are the only hitch in the choreographed order of the funeral procession. After the immediate family, the important person-ages scatter earth over the coffin, the members of the Politburo file past, then the heads of the army and the air force, then the Police Commissioner and the Director of Prisons, then the parliamentarians and the judges according to seniority.

∾

In the end, my words to Edna and my husband's family were no more than empty threats. I was per-suaded to stay, although I can no longer remember what empty promises I believed. I came to know the subtlety of the intonations of their language, that *chimbuzi* with the voice lowering over the middle and last syllable was a toilet, while *chimbudzi* with the extra *d* and the voice rising on the middle and the last syllable was a young goat. I learned to pronounce his children's names, and in the end did not need him, as he had done at first, to explain words to me.

'I named the first child Rwauya, meaning "death has come", and the second Muchagura to mean "you shall repent", and the last Muchakundwa, "you shall be defeated". They are messages for the white oppressors, warning signs to the white man.'

Thus had he stamped his patriotism on his children before leaving them with names that could mean nothing to the intended recipient of the messages, to the white man who chose to live in ignorance of native tongues. The white man has been conquered now, twice over, first in the matter of government, and now in the matter of the land that has been repossessed, but the children remain with their ominous names. I got to know them well because I replaced their mother after their father divorced her.

'There is no need for anything official,' my husband said. 'We are married under customary law, with no official papers. I will give her *gupuro* and she can take that to her family.' He picked out a pot with a red and yellow flower on it and gave it to her as a sign that he had divorced her. She died three years after that, but still, with her flowered pot and her early death, she got the better end of the bargain.

Like the worthless dogs that are his countrymen,

my husband believed that his penis was wasted if he was faithful to just one woman. He plunged himself into every bitch on heat, even that slut of a news-reader, the ruling party's First Whore, who lends the services of her vacuous beauty to their nightly distortions. She has been bounced from man to man, first as the mistress of a businessman who died with the red lips that spoke of his illness and then as the mistress of the Governor of the Central Bank, and after that, as the mistress of a minister without portfolio. Just like my husband, to salivate over other men's leavings.

∾

Muchakundwa and Muchagura are solemn in their dark suits. They live in California now, where they study on government scholarships. They have chosen to seek their fortunes far from this sovereign land that will never, a trillion trillion times never, be a colony again.

They left and Rwauya remained.

He would have been considered a failure, Rwauya, with his two O levels, but he is just the sort of person who thrives in this new dispensation, where to keep ahead is to go to every rally and chant every slogan. Even with all the patronage that is meant to oil his path to success, he has run down two butcheries and a bottle store, and, of six passenger buses, only one remains. He is full of schemes and ideas that never come to anything.

'*Ndafunga magonyeti*,' he said to his father and me, from which we understood that he was thinking of investing in haulage trucks. 'If I buy just two *magonyeti*, I will be okay.'

When the *magonyeti* scheme went down the primrose path along which went all others, he went from importing fuel and sugar to flying to Congo DRC and looting that country of cultural artefacts. And when Congo had been emptied of masks with cutout eyes and old wooden bowls and long-phallused fertility figures, he turned his thoughts to local stone sculpture.

'*Ndafunga zvematombo*,' he said, and began to export substandard chiselled bits of soapstone that were called Eagle or Spirit or Medium or Emptiness. 'If I make just two shipments, I will be okay.'

Now he wants his hands on the farm that my husband left. He arrived at the house four nights ago, looking like the death of his name, his eyes red from crapulence, with the mangy dreadlocks that are now a declaration of African authenticity if you believe that the authentic Africa is a place without combs or water to wash the hair. He gave me an embrace that lasted a fraction longer than it should have, his hand

13

brushing my bottom far from the shoulder where it should have been.

'You are looking very good, *Mainini*.'

I have learned to dispense with the niceties of social discourse with Rwauya and go straight to the heart of the matter. To my 'What is it you want?' he launched into a half-coherent account involving one of the six ministers without portfolio, the Minister's three nephews, one of whom was married to the daughter of the Chief of Police in Mazowe District who was in turn married to a niece of the Lands Minister.

'They have hired thugs to camp on the farm. Imagine, just two years after Father took it over from that Kennington,' he said. 'You have to do something to protect the farm. This is an invasion. They have no right to take it. My father died for this country. That farm is my birthright.'

'What is it that I can do?'

'*Izvi zvotoda* President. Ask to see the President. *Mainini*, you have access, just ask to see the President.'

❧

I could have talked to the President once, when he was still called the Prime Minister, before the Presidential Powers Amendment Act, before he ditched the Marxist austerity of his safari suits for pinstripes and gold cufflinks, before he married his second wife, Her Amazing Gracefulness, Our First Lady of the Hats. I was close to the inner circle then, close to his first wife, and we talked about women and education into the night.

'You are a coward,' she said to him. 'Isn't he a coward? I keep saying he should ban this demeaning polygamy.' His eyes laughed behind their glasses and he asked us how he could do this when the peasants were wedded to these arcane notions of life. The Minister of Justice talked about the difficulty of applying Marxist–Leninist principles in the context of African culture. 'The changes wrought by the Age of Majority Act show that, in the short term, law can be an instrument of social change, but ultimately, it is not the consciousness of man that determines his material being, but his material being that determines his consciousness. Law is a superstructure which must also wither when the state withers away.'

And we drank some more wine and argued about what would remain when the state withered away.

His wife gathered us to her in a small band of foreign women that their men had married in their exiles, some from as far away as Jamaica, England, Sweden, some from Ghana, Swaziland, South Africa.

15

We spoke English without feeling the need to apolo-
gise and drank wine and watched films at State House.
We were well educated, all of us: Bachelors of Arts and
Masters of Education, with three or four Doctors of
Medicine. Yet we seemed to accept that the world of
salaried work was closed to us as we raised children
and hosted parties at which the talk was dialectical
materialism and nation-building. When the World
Bank's focus moved to empowering civil society, the
donor money poured in and we undertook projects,
children's foundations, disability programmes,
women's empowerment, adult literacy campaigns.

'To help the nation-building process,' we said, but, in
reality, to keep ourselves busy and to close the chasm of
boredom that threatened to engulf us in its emptiness.

Then the First Lady died but before that there was
the Willowgate car scandal. 'Top Ministers Involved in
Illegal Sales of Government Cars', the newspaper head-
lines screamed, 'State House implicated in Willowgate'.

In the inner circle, we held our breaths and thought
heads would roll and the peasants and workers would
revolt, and demand an accounting. The only thing
that happened was the death of a minister in a
supremely self-indulgent act of suicide. His grave lies
over there behind the tomb of the Unknown Soldier.
In our band of foreign wives, we were shocked as our
friend and patron the First Lady was sucked to the

centre of the scandal. We became less shocked as she remained standing. The donor money poured in still, and we learned the benefits of creative accounting. We assured ourselves that the creative accounting did not matter because the peasants and the workers still got the benefit of the money.

She died, the First Lady, but even as his wife lay dying, the President kept an unofficial wife in a small house and our husbands also set up small houses and scattered their seed in every province. My husband and I were sent to a banana republic as the country's representatives while the nation forgot about his third scandal concerning government tenders.

We returned to an amnesiac nation, but our visits to State House were not as frequent. The unofficial wife in the small house had become the Second First Lady at State House. She wore hats of flying-saucer dimensions while cows sacrificed their lives so that she could wear pair upon pair of Ferragamo shoes.

'If only I could,' she said to the nation's orphans, 'I would really, really adopt you all.'

❧

A soldier steps out of the row of pallbearers with the flag folded in a neat triangular parcel. He salutes me before handing it to me. I let it sit in my lap with the stripes showing. I see the yellow and the green and the red and a bit of the black. The President looks into the distance.

᳕

'How can one man rule forever?' was the question that obsessed my husband before he died. 'Twenty-eight years, and still he wants to hang on?'

He joined in a plot to ensure that the next president would be from his province. There were secret meetings. They had come to the farm, the heavy-weights as the press calls them, referring to their assumed political influence, but the phrase could as well refer to their stomachs that require heavy lifting for all the copulation they seem to do with contestants and winners of beauty pageants. They plotted and schemed and the President got to know of their plots and schemes as he gets to know of everything. But the President was merciful; my husband's grovelling must have been so irritating that the only way to put an end to it would have been to extend the magnanimous hand of presidential pardon. He did not enjoy that forgiveness long because then he succumbed to a long illness, to use one of many presidential terms for death from Aids. He died, leaving me relieved that it had been years since I was a wife to him in any but the social sense.

᳕

'Forward, march.' The words are a strangled cry that seems to come from deep within the intestines of a soldier whose face is contorted from the effort of shouting them. This is followed by the rattle of a drum. The voice comes again and six soldiers march in formation and stand over the open grave.

There is a drum roll.

'Company, fire.'

The soldiers shoot into the air.

'Company, fire.'

More gunshots.

'Company, fire.'

And so on until twenty-one rounds have been shot into the air and the coffin has been sent off in the pomp and pageantry of a full military funeral. Tomorrow, the official newspaper will be full of a four-page photograph spread. They will say that my husband lay in state at Stoddard Hall before his coffin was loaded on to a gun carriage and travelled in a fifty-car cortège to the national shrine at Warren Hills, where a service from the official state priest was followed by an oration from the President, which was followed by a twenty-one-gun salute. There will be a full text of the President's speech. And for at least a week, the funeral will make up the entirety of the nightly news.

These are the ceremonies that give life to the ruling party's dream of perpetual rule, the pompous nothingness of the President's birthday celebrations, the state-sanctioned beauty pageants from which they choose new mistresses, the football matches with predetermined outcomes. The unity galas and musical 'bashes', the days of national prayer, and, above all these, the state funerals.

I wonder what the masses would say if they were to be told that they have gathered here to bury a bit of wood covering a sack filled with earth while the man we mourn lies in an unmarked grave.

∾

The newsreader who was my husband's mistress announced that my husband was to be made a national hero. The Politburo had declared him a hero to be buried at the national shrine. They did not tell me, his widow, of this decision and I had to hear it from his whore on the evening news. 'The shrine is where they lay the gallant sons who fought in the liberation struggle,' she added, helpfully.

What she does not say is that my husband is fortunate to have been awarded the status at all. Only those who had not disagreed with the President at the time of their deaths become heroes. A committee weighs the gallantry. It is sometimes necessary to upgrade those that were not gallant enough but sang well enough and danced high enough in the praise of the President to earn them a place there. My husband had been measured and the scales declared him worthy. He had never held a gun in his life. He knew nothing of the forests of Mozambique where the guerrillas trained. His main contribution to nation-building was to unite the nation in gossip over his five scandals. The scandals and his recent disloyalty have been discarded and all that matters is that he consolidated the gains of the liberation struggle by devotedly introducing the President by his full totem name.

In the end, they came to pay their respects and to talk about the funeral.

'His body will lie in state at Stoddard Hall,' the presidential spokesman said. 'He will proceed to Warren Hills for a full military burial.'

'Those were not his wishes,' I said. 'He wishes to be buried in his village.'

There was silence.

'His bones would not rest easy, he said, if he did not lie in the land in which he was born, where his ancestors are buried, and where he wants the bones of his children, and his children's children and their children in turn to lie with his when their time comes.

'It was his obsession in the end,' I continued. 'He believed that only if he lay in his home village would he find peace.'

21

I was sure that the reference to a potentially restless spirit would appeal to the atavistic instincts of the Cabinet members. They believe in the supernatural, after all, haunting traditional healers for success-guaranteeing potions and agitating for a law to punish witchcraft.

'We have no option but to go ahead with the funeral,' the spokesman insisted. 'The announcement has been made by the President himself; to go back would . . .' His voice trailed off but he did not need to finish the sentence. The President is not a man who loses face.

In the end, it was perhaps not so much the fear of my husband's *ngozi* spirit that made them treat me with respect as it was the necessity of avoiding the embarrassment that would result if I carried out my threat to go to the private press. They sent one emissary after another to talk to me, until they sent three heavyweights from the Politburo. After allusions to the family honour and talk of a personal triumph for my husband, came this plea: 'Think of how good it will be for his region.'

My husband was from the restive tribe in the south that sleeps and feeds and knows not the President. They carry a chip on their shoulder the size of their province. They do not have enough power, enough heroes at the national shrine. My husband's hero status would, they believed, quell the restive tribe, and still the fires that burned in the party over who will succeed the President. And in that realisation, I saw my future. I have no home in my own country to go to; everything that I have invested is here. I could choose to be an official widow to be trotted out at every commemoration of the heroes.

Or I could choose my own path.

'I want my husband's farm back,' I said, 'and I want it registered in title deeds in my name. I also want an uncontested seat in the new Senate.'

So the bargain was sealed: for a seat in the new Senate, and a farm in my own name, I would close my mouth and let them bury wood and earth in his name. They jumped at this; how could they not, when my husband had died in early August, which meant that they could have a real funeral on the very day in the middle of August that they commemorate men of the ruling party who have died still in agreement with the President. And so the spokesperson arranged everything, the coffin, the service, the switch after the lying in state at Stoddard Hall. He measured out exactly the precise kilograms of earth to represent my husband's dead weight. 'It must feel like the soldiers are carrying a real body,' he said.

∾

They have sounded the last post and fired the twenty-one-gun salute. I count slab upon slab of polished marble covering the desiccated bones of the dead heroes. One of them will soon cover the earth that is standing in for the flesh and bones of my husband.

There are many such secrets here, what the French call *les secrets de Polichinelle*, secrets that everyone may know but which may not be spoken. It is known that one of the heroes we buried recently was not the fine upstanding family man of the presidential speech but a concupiscent septuagenarian who died from a Viagra-induced heart attack while inside an underage girl. And it is known that the Governor of the Central Bank who has vowed to end illegal sales of fuel is himself involved in sales of fuel on the black market. And that the President . . . well, that which is not spoken or written down is not real.

Only the official truth matters, only that truth will be handed down through the history books for the children to learn. This they will learn: my husband is a national hero who lies at the Warren Hills. Warren Hills is the national shrine in a land presided over by the wisest of rulers. The land is one of plenty with happy citizens. The injustices of the past have been redressed to consolidate the gains of the liberation struggle. And in that happy land, I will be a new farmer and senator.

❧ An Elegy for Easterly ❧

It was the children who first noticed that there was something different about the woman they called Martha Mupengo. They followed her, as they often did, past the houses in Easterly Farm, houses of pole and mud, of thick black plastic sheeting for walls and clear plastic for windows, houses that erupted without City permission, unnumbered houses identified only by reference to the names of their occupants. They followed her past *Mai*James's house, *Mai*Toby's house, past the house occupied by Josephat's wife, and her husband Josephat when he was on leave from the mine, past the house of the newly arrived couple that no one really knew, all the way past the people waiting with plastic buckets to take water from Easterly's only tap.

'Where are you going, Martha Mupengo?' they sang.

She turned and showed them her teeth.

'May I have twenty cents,' she said, and lifted up her dress.

Giddy with delight, the children pointed at her nakedness. '*Hee, haana bhurugwa,*' they screeched. '*Hee*, Martha has no panties on, she has no panties on.'

However many times Martha Mupengo lifted her dress, they did not tire of it. As the dress fell back, it occurred to the children that there was something a little different, a little slow about her. It took a few seconds for Tobias, the sharp-eyed leader of Easterly's Under-Eights, to notice that the something different was the protrusion of the stomach above the thatch of dark hair.

'*Haa*, Martha Mupengo is swollen,' he shouted. 'What have you eaten, Martha Mupengo?'

The children took up the chorus. 'What have you eaten, Martha Mupengo?' They shouted as they followed her to her house in the far corner of Easterly. Superstition prevented them from entering. Tobias's chief rival Tawanda, a boy with four missing teeth and eyes as big as Tobias's ears were wide, threw a stick through the open doorway. Not to be outdone, Tobias picked up an empty baked beans can. He struck a metal rod against it, but even this clanging did not bring Martha out. After a few more failed stratagems, they moved on.

Their mouths and lungs took in the smoke-soaked smell of Easterly: smoke from outside cooking, smoke wafting in through the trees from the road-side where women roasted maize in the rainy season, smoke from burning grass three fields away, cigarette smoke. They kicked the empty can to each other until hunger and a sudden quarrel propelled Tobias to his family's house.

His mother *Mai*Toby sat at her sewing machine. Around her were the swirls of fabric, sky-blue, magnolia, buttermilk and bolts of white stuffing for the duvets that she made to sell. The small generator powering the sewing machine sent diesel fumes into the room. Tobias raised his voice above the machine.

'I am hungry.'

'I have not yet cooked, go and play.'

He sat in the doorway. He remembered Martha.

'Martha's stomach is swollen,' he said.

'Mmmm?'

'Martha, she is ever so swollen.'

'*Ho nhai?*'

He indicated with his arms and said again, 'Her stomach is this big.'

'*Hoo*,' his mother said without looking up. One half of her mind was on the work before her, and the other half was on another matter: should she put elaborate candlewick on this duvet, or should she

walk all the way to *Mai*James's to make a call to follow up on that ten million she was owed? *Mai*James
operated a phone shop from her house. She walked
her customers to a hillock at the end of the Farm and
stood next to them as they telephoned. On the
hillock, *Mai*James opened the two mobiles she had,
and inserted one SIM card after the other to see
which would get the best reception. Her phone was
convenient, but there was this: from *Mai*James came
most of the gossip at Easterly.

~

In her home, Martha slept.

Her name and memory, past and dreams, were
lost in the foggy corners of her mind. She lived in the
house and slept on the mattress on which a man
called Titus Zunguza had killed first his woman, and
then himself. The cries of Titus Zunguza's woman
were loud in the night. Help would have come, for
the people of Easterly lived to avoid the police. But
by the time Godwills Mabhena who lived next to
*Mai*James had crossed the distance to Titus
Zunguza's house, by the time he had roused a
sufficient number of neighbours to enter, help had
come too late. And when the police did come, they
were satisfied that it was no more than what it was.

Six months after the deaths, when blood still

showed on the mattress, Martha claimed the house simply by moving in. As the lone place of horror on Easterly, the house was left untouched; even the children acted out the terror of the murderous night from a distance.

They called her Martha because *Mai*James said that was exactly how her husband's niece Martha had looked in the last days when her illness had spread to her brain. 'That is how she looked,' *Mai*James said. 'Just like that, nothing in the face, just a smile, and nothing more.'

It was the children who called her Mupengo, Mudunyaz, and other variations on lunacy. The name Martha Mupengo stuck more than the others, becoming as much a part of her as the dresses of flamboyantly coloured material, bright with exotic flowers, poppies and roses and bluebells, dresses that had belonged to Titus Zunguza's woman and that hung on Martha's thin frame.

She was not one of the early arrivals to Easterly.

She did not come with those who arrived after the government cleaned the townships to make Harare pristine for the three-day visit of the Queen of England. All the women who walk alone at night are prostitutes, the government said – lock them up, the Queen is coming. There are illegal structures in the townships they said – clean them up. The townships are too full of people, they said, gather them up and put them in the places the Queen will not see, in Porta Farm, in Hatcliffe, in Dzivaresekwa Extension, in Easterly. Allow them temporary structures, and promise them real walls and doors, windows and toilets.

And so the government hid away the poverty, the people put on plastic smiles and the City Council planted new flowers in the streets.

Long after the memories of the Queen's visit had faded, and the broken arms of the arrested women were healed, Easterly Farm took root. The first wave was followed by a second, and by another, and yet another. Martha did not come with the first wave, nor with the next, nor with the one after that. She just appeared, as though from nowhere.

She did not speak beyond her request for twenty cents.

Tobias, Tawanda and the children thought this just another sign of madness, she was asking for something that you could not give. Senses, they thought, we have five senses and not twenty, until Tobias's father, *Ba*Toby, the only adult who took the trouble to explain anything, told them that cents were an old type of money, coins of different colours. In the days before a loaf of bread cost half a million dollars, he said, one hundred cents made one dollar. He took down an old tin and said as he opened it, 'We used the coins as recently as 2000.'

'Eight years years ago, I remember,' said an older child. 'The five cent coin had a rabbit, the ten cents a baobab tree. The twenty had . . . had . . . umm, *I* know . . . Beit Bridge.'

'Birchenough Bridge,' said *Ba*Toby. 'Beitbridge is one word, and it is a town.'

'The fifty had the setting sun . . .'

'Rising sun,' said *Ba*Toby.

'And the dollar coin had the Zimbabwe Ruins,' the child continued.

'Well done, good effort,' said *Ba*Toby. He spoke in the hearty tones of Mr Barwa, his history teacher from Form Three. He, too, would have liked to teach the wonders of Uthman dan Fodio's Caliphate of Sokoto and Tshaka's horseshoe battle formation, but providence in the shape of the premature arrival of Tobias had deposited him, grease under his nails, at the corner of Kaguvi Street and High Road, where he repaired broken-down cars for a living.

As he showed them the coins, he remembered a joke he had heard that day. He repeated it to the children. 'Before the President was elected, the Zimbabwe ruins were a prehistoric monument in Masvingo province. Now, the Zimbabwe ruins extend to the whole country.' The children looked at him blankly, before running off to play, leaving him to laugh with his whole body shaking.

The children understood that Martha's memory was frozen in the time before they could remember, the time of once upon a time, of good times that their parents had known, of days when it was normal to have more than leftovers for breakfast. 'We danced to records at Christmas,' *Ba*Toby was heard to say. 'We had reason to dance then, we had our Christmas bonuses.'

Like Martha's madness, the Christmas records and bonuses were added to the games of Easterly Farm, and for the children it was Christmas at least once a week.

❦

In the mornings, the men and women of Easterly washed off their sleep smells in buckets of water that had to be heated in the winter. They dressed in shirts and skirts ironed straight with coal irons. In their smart clothes, thumbing lifts at the side of the road, they looked like anyone else, from anywhere else.

The formal workers of Easterly Farm were a small number: the country had become a nation of informal traders. They were blessed to have four countries bordering them: to the north, Zambia, formerly one-Zambia-one-nation-one-robot-one-petrol-station,

Zambia of the joke currency had become the stop of choice for scarce commodities; to the east, Mozambique, their almost colony, *kudanana kwevanhu veMozambiki neZimbabwe*, reliant on their solidarity pacts and friendship treaties, on their soldiers guarding the Beira Corridor; this Mozambique was now the place to withdraw the foreign money not available in their own country; to the west, Botswana, how they had laughed at Botswana with no building taller than thirteen storeys, the same Botswana that now said it was so full of them that it was erecting a fence along the border to electrify their dreams of three meals a day; and, to the south, cupping Africa in her hands of plenty, Ndazo, *ku*South, Joni, Jubheki, Wenera, South Africa.

They had become a nation of traders.

So it was that in the mornings, the women of the markets rose early and caught the mouth of the rooster. In Mbare Musika they loaded boxes of leaf vegetables, tomatoes and onions, sacks of potatoes, yellow bursts of spotted bananas. They took omnibuses to Mufakose, to Kuwadzana and Glen Norah to stand in stalls and coax customers.

'One million for two, five million for six, only half a million.'

'Nice bananas, nice tomatoes, buy some nice bananas.'

They sang out their wares as they walked the streets.

'*Mbambaira, muriwo, ma*tomato, onion, *ma*banana, *ma*orange.'

The men and boys went to Siyaso, the smoke-laced second-hand market where the expectation of profit defied the experience of breaking even. In this section, hubcaps, bolts, nuts, adaptors, spanners. Over there, an entire floor given over to the mysterious bits, spiked and heavy, rusted and box-shaped, that give life to appliances. In the next, sink separators, plugs, cell-phone chargers. Under the bridge, cobblers making *manyatera* sandals out of disused tyres. The shoes were made to measure, 'Just put your foot here, *blaz*,' the sole of the shoe sketched out and cut out around the foot, a hammering of strips of old tyre onto the sole, and lo, fifteen-minute footwear. In Siyaso, it was not unknown for a man whose car had been relieved of its radio or hubcaps to buy them back from the man into whose hands they had fallen. At a discount.

On the other side of Mbare, among the *zhing-zhong* products from China, the shiny clothes spelling out cheerful poverty, the glittery tank tops and body tops imported in striped carrier bags from Dubai, among the Gucchii bags and Prader shoes, among the Louise Vilton bags, the boys of Muped-zanhamo competed to get the best customers.

'Sister, you look so smart. With this on you, you will be smarter still.'

'Leave my sister be, she was looking this way, this way, sister.'

'Sister, sister, this way.'

'This way, sister.'

'This way.'

'Sister.'

'My *si*.'

They spent the day away from Easterly Farm, in the city, in the markets, in Siyaso. They stood at street corners selling belts with steel buckles, brightly coloured Afro combs studded with mirrors, individual cigarettes smoked over a newspaper read at a street corner, boiled eggs with pinches of salt in brown paper. They passed on whispered rumours about the President's health.

'He tumbled off the stairs of a plane in Malaysia.'

'Yah, that is what happens to people who suffer from foot and mouth, people who talk too much and travel too much.'

At the end of the day, smelling of heat and dust, they packed up their wares and they returned to Easterly Farm, to be greeted again by Martha Mupengo.

'May I have twenty cents,' she said, and lifted up her dress.

❧

Josephat's wife was the first of the adults to recognise Martha's condition. She and Josephat, when he was home from the mine, lived in the house that had belonged to her aunt. It was five years since Josephat's wife had married Josephat. She had tasted the sound of her new identity on her tongue and liked it so much that she called herself nothing else. 'This is Josephat's wife,' she said when she spoke into the telephone on the hillock above the Farm. 'Hello, hello. It's Josephat's wife. Josephat's *wife*.'

'It is like she is the first woman in the entire world to be married,' *Mai*James said to *Mai*Toby.

'*Vatsva vetsambo*,' said *Mai*Toby. 'Give her another couple of years of marriage and she will be smiling on the other side of her face.'

On that day, Josephat's wife was walking slowly back into Easterly, careful not to dislodge the thick wad of cotton the nurses had placed between her legs. Like air seeping out of the wheels of a bus on the rocky road to Magunje, the joy was seeping out of the marriage. *Kusvodza*, they called it at the hospital, which put her in mind of *kusvedza*, slipping, sliding, and that is what was happening, the babies slipped and slid out in a mess of blood and flesh. She had moved to Easterly Farm to protect the unborn, fleeing from Mutoko where Josephat had brought her as a bride. After three miscarriages, she believed the tales of witchcraft that were whispered about Josephat's aunts on his father's side.

'They are eating my children,' she declared, when Josephat found her at his two-roomed house at Hartley Mine near Chegutu. She stayed only six months. After another miscarriage, she remembered the whispers about the foreman's wife, and her friend Rebecca who kept the bottle store.

'They are eating my children,' she said and moved to her aunt's house in Mbare. There she remained until the family was evicted and set up home in Easterly Farm. After another miscarriage, she said to her aunt, 'You are eating my children.'

Her aunt did not take this well. She had, after all, sympathised with Josephat's wife, even telling her of other people who might be eating her children. In the fight that followed, Josephat's wife lost a tooth and all the buttons of her dress. Then the younger brother of the aunt's husband had died. By throwing the dead brother's widow and her young family out of their house in Chitungwiza, the aunt and her husband acquired a new house, and Josephat's wife was left in Easterly.

In the evenings, she read from her Bible, her lips moving as she read the promises for the faithful. 'Is there any among you that is sick? Let him call for the elders of the Church; and let them pray over him, anointing him with oil in the name of the Lord. And the prayer of faith shall save the sick.'

From church to church she flitted, worshipping in township backrooms while drunken revellers roared outside, mosquitoes gorging on her blood in the open fields as she prayed among the white-clad, visiting prophets with shaven heads and hooked staffs who put their hands on her head and on her breasts. At the Sacred Church of the Anointed Lamb, at the Temple of God's Deliverance, at the Church of Our Saviour of Glad Tidings, she cried out her need in the language of tongues. She chased a child as her fellow penitents chased salvation, chased a path out of penury, chased away the unbearable heaviness of loneliness, sought some kind of redemption. And if the Lord remained deaf, that was because she had not asked hard enough, prayed hard enough, she thought.

She was walking past *Mai*Toby's house on the way to her own, when she remembered that *Mai*Toby had told her about a new church whose congregation prayed in the field near Sherwood Golf Course in Sentosa. 'You can't miss them,' *Mai*Toby had said. 'You go along Quendon, until you reach the Tokwe flats. They worship under a tree on which hangs a big square flag; it has a white cross on a red background.'

It means taking three commuter omnibuses,

Josephat's wife thought. First, the omnibus to Mabvuku, then one to town. She would have to walk for fifteen or so minutes from Fourth Street to Leopold Takawira, take an omnibus to Avondale and walk for another forty-five minutes to Sentosa.

I will rise at five, she thought, *and catch the mouth of the rooster.*

She remembered that she had not been able to reach her husband at the mine to tell him of yet another miscarriage. That thought directed her feet towards *Mai*James's house. It was then that she saw Martha. The woman did not need to lift her dress to reveal the full contours of pregnancy. The sight reached that part of Josephat's wife's spirit that still remained to be crushed. She ran past Martha, they brushed shoulders, Martha staggered a little, but Josephat's wife moved on.

'May I have twenty cents,' Martha called out after her.

∾

In her dreams, Josephat's wife turned to follow the sound of a crying child. At Hartley Mine, her husband Josephat eased himself out of the foreman's wife's friend Rebecca who kept the bottle store. He turned his mind to the increasing joylessness of his marriage bed. Before, his wife had opened all of herself to him,

41

had taken all of him in, rising, rising, rising to meet him, before falling, falling down with him.

Now it was only after prayers for a child that she lay back, her eye only on the outcome. *It is a matter of course that we will have children*, Josephat had thought when they married. *Boys, naturally. Two boys, and maybe a girl.*

He no longer cared what came. All he wanted was to stop the pain. He eased himself out of Rebecca, lay back, and thought of his wife in Easterly.

∾

The winter of the birth of Martha's child was a winter of broken promises. The government promised that prices would go down and salaries up. Instead, the opposite happened. The opposition promised that there would be protests. Instead they bickered over who should hold three of the top six positions of leadership. From the skies fell *chimvuramabwe*, hailstones of frozen heat that melted on the laughing tongues of Easterly's children. The children jabbed fingers at the corpses of the frogs petrified in the stream near the Farm. The water tap burst.

*Mai*James and *Ba*Toby argued over whether this winter was colder than the one in the last year but one of the war. *Mai*James spoke for the winter of the war, *Ba*Toby for the present winter. 'You were no higher than Toby *uyu*,' *Mai*James said with no rancour. 'What can you possibly remember about that last winter but one?'

It was the government that settled the matter.

'Our satellite images indicate that a warm front is expected from the Eastern Highlands. The warm weather is expected to hold, so pack away those heaters and jerseys. And a very good night to you from your friendly meteorologist, Stan Mukasa. You are listening to *nhepfenyuro yenyu*, Radio Zimbabwe. Over to Nathaniel Moyo now, with *You and Your Farm*.'

This meant that *Ba*Toby was right. If the government said inflation would go down, it was sure to rise. If they said there was a bumper harvest, starvation would follow. 'If the government says the sky is blue, we should all look up to check,' said *Ba*Toby.

That winter brought the threat of more evictions. There had been talk of evictions before, there was nothing new there. They brushed it aside and put more illegal firewood on their fires. Godwills Mabhena who lived next to *Mai*James burnt his best trousers.

❧

By the middle of that winter, all of Easterly knew that Martha was expecting a child. The men made ribald comments about where she could have found a man to do the deed. The women worked to convince themselves that it was a matter external to Easterly, to themselves, to their men. 'You know how she disappears for days on end sometimes,' said *Mai*Toby. 'And you know how wild some of those street kids are.'

'Street kids? Some of them are men.'

'My point exactly.'

'Should someone not do something, I don't know, call someone, maybe the police?' asked the female half of the couple whom nobody really knew.

'Yes, you are very right,' said *Mai*James. 'Someone should do something.'

'That woman acts like we are in the suburbs,' *Mai*James later said to *Mai*Toby. 'Police? Easterly? *Ho-do!*' They clapped hands together as they laughed.

'*Haiwa*, even if you call them, would they come? It took what, two days for them to come that time when Titus Zunguza . . .'

'*Ndizvo*, they will not come if *we* have a problem, what about for Martha?'

'And even if they did, what then?'

The female half of the couple that no one really knew remembered that her brother's wife attended the same church as a woman who worked in social welfare. 'You mean Maggie,' her brother's wife said. 'Maggie moved *ku*South with her husband long back. I am sure by now her husband drives a really good car, *mbishi chaiyo*.'

She got the number of the social department from the directory. But the number she dialled was out of service, and after three more attempts, she gave it up. *There is time enough to do something*, she thought.

And when the children ran around Martha and laughed, 'Go and play somewhere else,' *Mai*Toby scolded them. 'Did your mothers not teach you to respect your elders? And as for you, *wemazinzeve*,' she turned to Tobias. 'Come and wash yourself.'

The winter of Martha's baby was the winter of Josephat's leave from the mine. It was Easterly's last winter.

❧

On the night that Martha gave birth, Josephat's wife walked to Easterly from a praying field near Mabvuku. She did not notice the residents gathered in clusters around their homes. Only when she walked past Martha's house did the sounds of Easterly reach her. Was that a moan, she wondered. Yes, that sounded like a cry of pain. Without thinking, she walked-ran into Martha's house. By the light of the moon falling through the plastic sheeting, she saw Martha, naked on her mattress, the head of her baby between her legs.

'I'll get help,' Josephat's wife said. 'I'll get help.'

She made for the door. Another moan stopped her and she turned back. She knelt by the mattress and looked between Martha's legs. 'Twenty cents,' Martha said and fainted.

Josephat's wife dug into the still woman and grabbed a shoulder. Her hand slipped. She cried tears of frustration. Again, she dug, she pulled, she eased the baby out. Martha's blood flowed onto the mattress. 'Tie the cord,' Josephat's wife said out loud and tied it.

She looked around for something with which cut the cord. There was nothing, and the baby almost slipped from her hands. Through a film of tears she chewed on Martha's flesh, closing her mind to the taste of blood, she chewed and tugged on the cord until the baby was free. She wiped the blood from her mouth with the back of her hand. The baby cried, she held it to her chest, and felt an answering rise in her breasts. She sobbed out laughter. Her heart loud in her chest, she took up the first thing she saw, a poppy-covered dress, and wrapped the baby in it.

In her house she heated water and wiped the baby clean. She dressed it in the clothes of the children who had slipped from her. She put the baby to breast and he sucked on air until both fell asleep. This was the vision that met Josephat when he returned after midnight. 'Whose child is that?'

'God has given me this child,' she said.

In the half-light Josephat saw his wife's face and his stomach turned to water. 'I will go to the police,' he said. 'You cannot snatch a child and expect me to do nothing.'

His wife clutched the baby closer. 'This is God's will. We cannot let Martha look after it. How can we let her look after a child?'

'What are you talking about, who is Martha?'

'Martha Martha, I left her in her house, she gave birth to it. She can't look after it, this is God's will.'

Josephat blundered out of the room. He knew with certainty that it was just as he thought. Ten months before he had arrived home, and found his wife not there. 'She has gone to an all-night prayer session,' a neighbour said. A wave of anger and repulsion washed over him. He had only this and the next night before he was to go back to the mine.

A wasted journey, he thought.

He had gone to the beer garden in Mabvuku. The smell of his wife was in the blankets when he returned, but she wasn't home. The hunger for a woman came over him. He left his house to urinate and relieved himself against the wall through the pain of his erection. A movement to the right caught his eye. He saw the shape of a woman. His mind turned immediately to thoughts of sorcery. He lit a cigarette and in the flare of the match saw the mad woman. 'May I have twenty cents,' she said, and lifted her up dress.

He had followed the woman to her house in the corner, grappled her to the ground, forced himself on her, let himself go, and in that moment came to himself. 'Forgive me,' he said, 'forgive me.'

He did not look at her until she said, 'May I have twenty cents.' He looked at her smiling face with horror; he fell over his trousers and backwards into the door. He pulled up his trousers as he ran and did not stop running until he reached his house. 'It is not me,' he had said again and again. 'This is not me.'

He lit a cigarette. There was a smell of burning filter. He had lit the wrong end. He bargained with God, he bargained with the spirits on both his mother's and his father's sides. He bargained with himself. He would touch no woman other than his wife. He would not leave her, even if she never bore him a child. And even as he later gave in to Rebecca, to Juliet, and the others, he told himself that these others meant nothing at all.

❧

Josephat found Martha lying on the floor on her back. He raised her left arm, it fell back. He covered her body with a blanket, and left the house. Snatches of conversation reached his ears from the group gathered around *Ba*Toby. For the first time he realised that Easterly was still awake, unusually so; it was well after midnight and yet here were people gathered around in knots in the moonlight. He moved close, he had to know.

'They were at Union Avenue today, they took all the wares.'

'They just threw everything in the back of the lorries.'

'Didn't care what they broke. Just threw everything.'

'In Mufakose it was the same, they destroyed everything.'

'Siyaso is gone, Mupedzanhamo too.'

'Union Avenue flea market.'

'*Kwese neku*Africa Unity, it is all cleared.'

'Even *kuma*surburbs, they attacked Chisipite market.'

'My cousin-brother said they will come for the houses next.'

'They would not dare.'

'*Hanzi* there are bulldozers at Porta Farm as we speak.'

'If they can destroy Siyaso . . .'

'But they can't destroy Siyaso.'

'That is not possible,' said *Ba*Toby. 'I will not believe it.'

'I was there,' Godwills Mabhena said. 'I was there.'

'You men, the only thing you know is to talk and talk,' *Mai*James said. 'Where are you when action is required? Where were you when they took down Siyaso? *Nyararazvako.*' The last word of comfort was directed to the crying child on her hip. His mother was one of three women arrested in Mufakose, two for attempting to take their clothes off in protest, the third, the child's mother, for clinging to her box of produce even as a truncheon came down, again, again, on her bleeding knuckles. The child sniffled into *Mai*James's bosom.

'I will not believe it,' *Ba*Toby said again.

∾

In his house Josephat took down a navy-blue suitcase and threw clothes into it. His wife held the baby in a tender lock and crooned a lullaby that Josephat's own mother had sung to him.

'*Your child will not be consoled, sister.*'

'We are leaving,' he said.

'*She cries for her mother, gone away.*'

'We have to pack and leave.'

'*Gone away, to Chidyamupunga.*'

'The bulldozers are coming.'

'*Chidyamupunga, cucumbers are rotting.*'

'We have to leave now.'

'*Cucumbers are rotting beyond Mungezi.*'

'Ellen, please.'

She looked up at him. He swallowed. Her smile in the half-light put him in mind of Martha. 'We have to leave,' he said. He picked up an armful of baby clothes. He held them in his hands for a moment, then stuffed them into the suitcase and closed it.

'It is time to go,' he said. As they walked, to Josephat's mind came the words of his mother's lullaby.

> *Cucumbers are rotting beyond Mungezi.*
> *Beyond Mungezi there is a big white knife,*
> *A big white knife to cut good meat,*
> *To cut good meat dried on a dry bare rock . . .*

They stole out of Easterly Farm and into the dawn.

When the morning rose over Easterly, not even the children noticed Martha's absence. They were running away from the bulldozers. It was only when Josephat and his wife had almost reached Chegutu that the bulldozers, having razed the entire line of houses from *Mai*James to *Ba*Toby, having crushed beneath them the house from which Josephat and his wife had fled, and having razed that of the new couple that no one really knew, finally lumbered towards

51

Martha's house in the corner and exposed her body, stiff in death, her child's afterbirth wedged between her legs.

∾ The Annexe Shuffle ∾

Emily sees Ezekiel shake his arms and hands around his head. Ezekiel is haunted by the buzzing of a thousand phantom mosquitoes. They fly close to his ear; it is always the same ear, the right ear. He swipes at them but this only increases their agitation. He longs to hit one, just one, and see the satisfying streak of blood across the wall. Sometimes he slaps a hand against one, again, again, but he hits nothing but the wall and, more often, himself.

He has to be bandaged often.

In between the buzzing mosquitoes, he says that he hears other sounds: shouting men dressed as soldiers, the dry crackle of the straw on burning huts, screaming children, crying women. More frequent and disturbing than that is this, the high intermittent buzz of the thousand mosquitoes. To keep their noise out of his head, Ezekiel sings a song that Emily remembers from Sunday school:

'Father Abraham, please send Lazarus
To rescue me, I am burning in this fire.
Yuwi maiwe yuwi,
Yuwi maiwe yuwi.
Please send Lazarus, to rescue me
I am dying in this heat.'

And when he screams 'Abraham, Abraham' at least twenty times, the mosquitoes are still.

His shouting puts him in conflict with Sister Hedwig. She raps him sharply on the head with her knuckles. He stops screaming, and whispers 'Abraham, Abraham' from near the window, close to where Emily stands. She sees him trembling and instinctively puts a hand on his shoulder. They stand in silence looking out at Second Street Extension, at the embassy houses of Belgravia and the golf course across the road. Through the metal grille and the mesh wire, through the reinforced windows that separate them from the outside, they can see small figures on the eighteenth green.

Only outside this window is there change, yet even there a repetitive pattern asserts itself. On Second Street Extension, the cars, buses, emergency taxis are filled with people going about the business of living, the occupants within unaware of the gazes without. One time, two times, five times a day she sees the vans and cars from her suspended life. Up and down goes the little green bus, moving between the city centre and the university. 'University of Zimbabwe', a white station wagon says in blue lettering, 'Faculty of Law'. The car is so close that she can make out the faculty motto below the university crest: *fiat justitia ruat coelum*. The motto is more than just the words of Caesoninus on a crest, it is a song in her soul, the reason she is a law student, the meaning she wants to give to her life. 'Let justice be done though the heavens fall,' she says aloud. Outside, the traffic, golf course, the houses. Inside, the Annexe shuffle.

❦

They bring Emily to Dr Chikara, the Dean of Students on one side, the warden of Swinton Hostel on the other. Dr Chikara is not who she expected. His office is an empty space with nothing on the walls. There are no books by Freud and Jung. There is no couch in sight. He does not talk about the id or the ego. Instead, from behind his government-issue desk, he directs her to a government-issue chair.

He smokes Kingsgate cigarettes, one after the other.

He writes down everything she says.

'Canst thou minister to a mind diseased?' she asks him. 'Pluck from the memory a rooted sorrow?'

He writes this down.

'May I have a cigarette,' she says, without a question mark.

'Do you smoke?' he asks, with a question mark.

'I do now,' she says as she lights one of his cigarettes. She coughs out smoke through teary eyes.

He writes that down too.

'I am sending you to the Annexe,' he says, 'the mental wing at Parirenyatwa Hospital.'

The words *mental* and *hospital* combine to produce a loud clanging in her mind.

'I am not mad,' she says.

'No, of course you are not mad,' he says. 'Madness has nothing to do with it. You only need rest, all you need is rest.'

Emily is pliant, obedient, she needs rest. The warden calls her a taxi, to be paid for by the university. 'I am visiting a friend,' she tells the driver, even though he has not asked. Inside the Annexe, the door shuts behind her. A man in a striped robe walks the slow walk that puts her in mind of the undead of film and television. In his face is vacant possession.

'Do you have *Parade*, sister?' he slurs.

She turns towards the door but there is no handle on the inside.

'I am not supposed to be here,' she says, 'let me out, let me out.'

'Sister, may I have *Parade*?' the man says, and touches her face. The man attracts others, and two women shuffle towards her, with faces as empty as his. Like a persistent interloper, the rhyme from Stephen King's *Tommyknockers* reverberates in her mind. *Late last night and the night before, Tommyknockers, Tommyknockers, knocking at the door.* The door won't open, and she bangs on it to escape the shuffling figures in their striped robes. A nurse comes to her, face clouded with concern.

'Is it not that you are the girl from the university?' the nurse asks in Shona. 'Is it not that Dr Chikara sent you here?'

'No, no,' Emily says in English, 'let me out.'

I want to go out, don't know if I can.

'Are you not the one we are expecting?' the nurse asks again.

'I am lost,' Emily says, 'so sorry, so lost, I should not be here.'

I am so afraid of the Tommyknocker man.

The door opens and she stumbles out.

❧

In her room on P corridor at Swinton, she announces to no one in particular: 'I am going to keep a journal. I am going to write down everything that happens to me. Today I ate my banana,' she says, 'so I will write that down.'

'I ate my banana,' she writes.

Only it comes out 'I hate my banana', and, seeing

this, she laughs. Then she sees that this is not so funny, this is, in fact, a sign that everything is against her, she can't even trust her own pen, her own hand, her own thoughts, her very actions betray her, everything is against her, everything is wrong, so wrong, nothing will ever be right again.

It is as she cries that the Dean of Students and the warden enter her room to take her back to the Annexe. 'I know my rights,' she says through her tears. 'I am a law student.'

They brush away her law studies like an inconvenient fly.

'Your father said we can section you,' they say.

The force of her father's will moves across the country from Bulawayo to Harare. It takes the route that Emily herself takes to get to university each term, past Gweru, Kadoma, Chegutu. The force travels along the Bulawayo Road and propels her from her bed to pack a small bag. Pens and notebook, her new diary. Three changes of underwear, three T-shirts, two pairs of jeans. One book: *The Origin of the Family, Private Property and the State.*

∾

Her clothes are not wanted here, they remain in her bag. She wears a striped gown with the many-wash-faded letters ANNEXE ANNEXE ANNEXE all over it. She is branded across her breast, on her right arm, above her knees, across her back. She is small, Emily. The gowns are supposed to be one-size-fits-all but hers is so big that she feels like she is in a tent. In the window, she catches her reflection. She cannot see herself. MockingNurseMatilda takes down her particulars. Name, age, race, religion, height, weight. She asks Emily what tribe she belongs to.

'This is what slows progress in this country,' Emily screams. 'The notion of tribe is a patronising Western construction,' she adds when they have restrained her. 'The Goths, Vandals and Visigoths, those were tribes, they talk about Serbian nationalism, but African tribalism. I do not have a tribe, I belong to the nation.'

They force her onto the bed.

'I am a student,' she weeps. 'A university student.'

'Hedwig is a Catholic Sister, Ezekiel is an army sergeant, Sonia there manages a hotel,' MockingNurseMatilda says. 'Welcome to the Annexe, my dear, we welcome students too.'

Emily reads aloud from the *Origin of the Family*. A wave of gratitude washes over her. These men, Marx and Engels, Karl and Friedrich, dead and white, they get it, they really, really get it. 'In the first place, sexual love assumes that the person loved returns the love; to this extent the woman is on an equal footing with the man. Secondly, our sexual love has a degree of intensity and duration which makes both lovers feel that non-possession and separation are a great, if not the greatest, calamity; to possess one another, they risk high stakes, even life itself.'

She cries herself to sleep. She wakes to find a Coloured girl staring at her and smiling as she plays with the beads at the ends of the braids on Emily's hair. 'Feel my baby,' the Coloured girl says.

Her name is Estelle, and she is a star rising high above the reaches of all that is ordinary and elemental. Nothing can touch her, and nothing does.

'Feel my baby,' she says again, eyes closed. She places Emily's hand on her stomach, chopping-board flat. 'He will be born tomorrow.'

'Ralph.' Estelle says the name like she is tasting its sound.

'Ralph,' she repeats.

'That is what I'll call him, Ralph, like the Karate Kid.'

Together Emily and Estelle look out onto Second Street Extension where up and down goes the little green bus.

∾

In the Annexe, she finds that she is not the only one who is not mad.

'I am not mad,' says Ezekiel.

'And I am not mad,' says Estelle.

'Why do you look at me as though I am mad?' asks Hedwig and hits Ezekiel on the head. No one is mad except the nurses with their faces out of focus, they are gone and there they are again, with their large ears and large hands that grab and say she needs rest. They give her three small pills, one orange, one square and white, one round and white. She is happy that it is NiceNurseLindiwe and not MockingNurseMatilda who helps her to a bed. There is something Emily has to tell her, something important, terribly, desperately important. It is the most important thing she has ever said to anyone. She clutches NiceNurseLindiwe's arm and looks into her eyes. 'Beware the Jabberwock, my son,' she says. 'The jaws that bite, the claws that catch. Beware the Jubjub bird, and shun the frumious Bandersnatch.'

∽

Ezekiel sits in the corner away from the windows. Concentrated, he won't show anyone what he is doing. He reveals his work eventually, shyly, a pencil drawing of the Taj Mahal. The domes and columns are delicately fragile in black and white. 'That's a building in India,' he says. 'I saw it in a book.' The next time that Ezekiel screams 'Abraham, Abraham',

Sister Hedwig tears the drawing and the Taj Mahal flutters in seven torn pieces to the floor. Ezekiel does nothing but sit and draw another. He gives it to Emily. If possible, it is even more beautiful than the first one. 'It is the most beautiful thing that I have seen,' she says, and means it. She cries, for no reason. Ezekiel puts his hand on her shoulder and smiles. Together, they look outside the window. She persuades him to sing a new song. She chooses a Sunday school song that also features Abraham.

> *'Father Abraham has many sons*
> *Has many sons, has Father Abraham*
> *I am one of them and so are you.*
> *So let us praise the Lord.'*

Up and down Second Street Extension goes the little green bus.

∾

Hedwig, Emily, Estelle, Ezekiel. And Sonia, the resident white. Her hospital towel is twisted in a turban about her head. She smokes blue Madison, regally, she holds the cigarette away from her as she says to Emily, 'You speak English well. Very well, for an African.' She gives Emily her cigarettes. The blue Madison is not harsh on the throat like Dr Chikara's Kingsgate. Emily smokes one, five, this is the beginning of addiction, here in the Annexe.

And there is *Ma*Bheki in her corner.

Emily has learned to stay away from *Ma*Bheki. Her madness is of a malevolent bent, an ungentle madness that requires restraints, and not just the pills, orange and white, square and round.

'I want my meat,' *Ma*Bheki screams.

She has devoured all of her babies, she says, she is particularly fond of the flesh of her boy children. A peculiar hunger comes over her when she sees a male child, she says, she feels a compulsion to feed. She looks at Ezekiel as she talks, and Emily sings him the new Abraham song until he is calm. *Ma*Bheki is not long at the Annexe, her madness calls for rigour of the kind that the Annexe cannot deliver. They strap her to take her out of the Annexe, out of Harare and out of Mashonaland to Ingutsheni, the oldest, the biggest mental hospital in the country, Ingutsheni, the constant rebuke in the ears of the young: don't talk like you are at Ingutsheni. Before Ingutsheni was a mental hospital, it was a lunatic asylum, and there *Ma*Bheki's voice will join those of the dangerously mad, the criminally insane.

*Ma*Bheki bares her teeth and her eyes meet Emily's.

'I want my meat,' she says, and the door closes behind her.

In the moment that the door closes on *Ma*Bheki, Emily sees the trajectory of her own life: from the casual, almost conversational question, how many Disprin would you take to kill yourself, overheard by Anna the sub-warden, who puts the university machinery into operation by relaying the question to the warden who relays it to the Dean of Students who relays the question to Dr Chikara, who relays it to her parents who insist that she be sectioned in the Annexe. She grasps this much: she is here, not because she asked the question but because someone overheard her ask the question. Depending on whether she asks that question again, or, more precisely, depending on how loudly she asks it, her life could go either way, to the little green bus up Second Street Extension towards Bond Street, Pendennis and the university, or the other way, turning where Second Street meets Julius Nyerere Way to go past the National Gallery and the Monomotapa Crowne Plaza, past Town House and all the way to the railway station to take the night train to Ingutsheni.

Emily forces herself to be normal.

She stops speaking in poetry and quotations. She puts aside Marx and Engels. Inside herself, she recites 'Jabberwocky' and 'Macavity'. *Twas brillig, and the slithy toves did gyre and gimble in the wabe. All mimsy were the borogoves, and the mome raths outgrabe. His brow is deeply lined in thought, his head is highly domed. You would know him if you saw him for his eyes are sunken in.*

How many Disprin does it take to kill yourself, she asks. She calculates just how many would be required, four boxes, five boxes, maybe even ten boxes. She will drink them with vodka, drink them with Mazoe mixed with club soda. She does a comparative evaluation, Norolon versus Disprin. On a balance of probabilities, on the evidence of the gory newspaper tales of Norolon-induced abortions that end up killing both foetus and mother, Norolon would be more effective.

Outside herself, she helps to distribute the toast and tea in the mornings. Outside herself, she stares outside the window in the afternoon, careful not to sit there for too long. In her journal, she writes bright entries, with exclamation marks, about her future outside the Annexe. 'I am going to Oxford!' she writes, 'I am going be a Rhodes Scholar!'

The evening pills empty her thoughts.

In the evening, she does the Annexe shuffle.

❧

And then, just like that, Dr Chikara says she can go back to her life. She and Ezekiel sing 'Father Abraham' one more time, three more times, seven more times. Estelle joins in. Hedwig conducts them, insisting that they stand in a choir formation. Sonia applauds. MockingNurseMatilda shakes her head when she sees them. 'The choir of the mad,' she says to the orderlies, but there is no malice in her voice.

Emily walks out of the door that has no handle on the inside. The last thing she sees is Ezekiel saying 'Abraham, Abraham' while Hedwig hits him on the head. She stands on Second Street Extension, and waits for the little green bus. She re-enters academe to nudges and whispered comments. She is the subject of clever jokes, lawyer jokes.

'She is not a fit and proper person,' says one.

'She is not a competent witness,' says another.

'She qualifies under the Mental Health Act,' says a third.

She is so concentrated on being normal that thoughts of Disprin versus Norolon recede to that part of her mind that is most active in fantasy. Her exam results are stellar; she achieves seven firsts in one year. She receives the University Book Prize three years in a row. Her essay on the presidential pardon and the rule of law is published in the *Legal Forum*. But for the rest of her three years at the university, she is known as Emily from Law who tried to kill herself when her boyfriend, Gwinyai from Engines, dumped her for Lydia, the tall, skinny girl from

Sociology. Even first years that were not there pass on the story, which grows with each telling and retelling.

'She climbed a tree, that tree opposite the Students' Union.'

'She swallowed forty tablets.'

'She was found unconscious on the floor.'

'Naked.'

'She threw herself in front of her boyfriend's car.'

'Not her boyfriend's car, it was the Dean of Students' car.'

'He took her to hospital.'

'Hospital, *chii*, they put her in a car, on a bus, on a train, on a plane, to Ingutsheni.'

The pinnacle of absurdity is reached in Emily's third year when a first-year girl, seeing Emily, and not knowing who she is, asks her, 'Is it true that that Emma girl from Law tried to kill herself in my room?'

It is true; FirstYearGirl sleeps in Emily's old room on P.

'Don't believe everything you hear,' Emily says. 'It happened on Q corridor.' She says this to be kind, but the next time that FirstYearGirl sees Emily, it is with knowledge in her eyes. The Emma Girl from Law of legend has become the in-the-flesh Emily walking towards her. She moves to the other side and walks past Emily without meeting her eyes.

Among the whispers and the pointing, Emily

moves as the incarnation of the walking mad. Though she relearns how to be normal, there is incontrovertible evidence that the true lesson of her experience is lost on her: she falls in love again, just as carelessly, almost as excessively, this time with a rugby-playing Economics student known to everyone but his mother as Tuggs. 'I like you babes, I really do,' Tuggs says, 'but this can't go on, you know that. What if you go all crazy on me like you did with that guy from Engines?' This rejection is the first of many post-Gwinyai heartbreaks; but she learns this: no heartbreak will ever again be sharp enough to send her over the edge and to the Annexe.

Each heartbreak is a little death, all the same.

Up and down she goes in the little green bus, always sitting on the right so that she looks out at the golf course and not at the Annexe opposite. In her drawer with her diary and fevered poems, she keeps Ezekiel's picture of the Taj Mahal. In her final year at university, she is three-quarters of the way from the Annexe and a quarter of the distance from Oxford. There is nothing to do but celebrate the end of exams, the approach of Christmas, going home, the unwritten future.

It is Friday evening, and she is with Fadz and Sihle

and Kenny and Lindy buying mushroom burgers at Chicken Inn. They will tumble into Fadz's battered Beetle and go on to a night of clubbing at Circus. They have been drinking vodka, and they laugh at the smallest thing. She comes out onto Inez Terrace, in mid-laugh, and there, holding a box of fried chicken is Ezekiel. His smile is wide as he moves towards her. He says something, a greeting, but all she hears is, 'Abraham, Abraham,' as up and down goes the little green bus. She turns away. He sees her pretending and she sees him seeing. She pretends not to see the shadow that falls across his face.

∽ Something Nice from London ∽

The little boy in the orange shirt tells me that his grandmother says that his mummy is bringing him something nice from London. 'Your mummy will bring you something nice from London too,' he asserts, with all the gravity of a child whose concerns coincide with those of the world. He runs off before I can reply, and I watch him tear up and down the observation platform that overlooks the arrival hall of our airport. The Chinese built this airport when the old one became too small for the tourists that poured into the country in their thousands. No tourists visit us now. Our almost total isolation means that we have no camera-toting, free-spending visitors to pour dollars and pounds, euros, yen and yuan into our empty coffers. We have an international airport in name only; the twice-weekly flight to and from London provides the only direct link we have to the world beyond our continent.

We wait for the Friday morning flight from London, as I stand with my mother, my brother Jonathan and his wife Mukai, and watch through the transparent glass of the observation platform. Our sombre faces are out of place, surrounded by those that smile in anticipation, with mouths that laugh and fingers that point out to children, there they are, there she is, he is here at last; they arrived on time. My mother stares unseeing at the passengers below us who crane their necks to look up at the platform, anxious to catch a glimpse of a familiar face, arms waving and jangling with bracelets, faces broad with smiles. They have made an effort for the flight, the women in manicured wigs and weaves, their England clothes fitting well, their skin lightened by years, and maybe even by just as little as six months of living out of the heat and stress of poverty. Those receiving them have also made an effort, or maybe it is not such an effort. They will have been happy to put aside their quiet desperation to wear the shining joy of welcome. For these passengers bring with them more than their loved selves, they bring something nice from London, the foreign money that will be traded on the black market and guarantee a few more months of survival.

We wait two hours before Jonathan confirms with the airline that Peter is not on the flight. The flight from Johannesburg arrives next, and we resign ourselves to returning home. We exchange no words as we walk back to the car park; my mother between Jonathan and Mukai, and me two steps behind. The car radio bursts into life as soon as Jonathan starts the engine. A voice reminds us that the land is ours, it will not be taken from us again; the country will never be a colony again. The message is repeated three times in the twenty minutes that it takes Jonathan to drive us home. In between the repeated message there are songs of histrionic patriotism, including one that I have not heard before in which the singer extols the President as a direct descendant of Christ and implores the Almighty to grant long life to him, to his wife and to all his children.

❧

As Jonathan winds into the open gate to the driveway of our garden, the women gathered in the front of the house see us and begin a persistent keening. They are echoed by more women who pour out of the house, jumping in little paroxysms of grief. They cry out, 'Peter *woye, nhai* Peter, Peter *kani*, Peter, Peter, Peter, Peter.' They tear the air with a thousand Peters, each one a crescendo building onto the next. My paternal aunt *Mai*Lisa outdoes them all as she hops first on one leg, then the other, bends low from her waist, raises herself and puts her hands on her head and wails with her face to the sky, tears streaming from her eyes as underarm sweat dampens the light-coloured fabric of her dress. She nearly fells my mother as she embraces her. She almost knocked me over yesterday, so when I see her propelling herself towards me, I head off and envelop myself in the keening of the collected family daughters-in-law. They are the official criers, and they begin the ritual chanting and invocation of Peter's name.

'We will not see him again, *uhuu*.'

'Why have you left us, oh my father, *yuwi*?'

'You have left us alone, and bereft, *yuwi*.'

'Regard your mother, she is bereft and inconsolable.'

'You are too cruel, Peter, come back Peter, *kani*.'

'Who shall care for us now that you have left, *uhuu*?'

The men of the family follow behind, maintaining a distance from this rigorous mourning, this business of women. The sound of grieving tears the air until the moment is over and they want to know what happened.

'Peter's body did not arrive,' Jonathan explains.

This does not satisfy the relatives, and the questions remain. *Mai*Lisa is silent now that explanations are required. She had passed on the message from her daughter Lisa in England, Peter is coming home, she said. Now that Peter is not here, and we want to know what happened, she discovers that she is needed in the kitchen and is now commanding the family daughters-in-law. Their non-agnatic status in the family means that not only are theirs the lungs that provide the loudest mourning, theirs are also the hands that cook and clean at family gatherings. We can get nothing from her beyond 'I know only what I have told you. Lisa is there. Why estimate the length of a snake using the bark of a tree when the creature is right there for you to measure?'

❧

Lisa calls that evening to explain that when she had told her mother that Peter would be on the morning flight, she had meant only that there was merely a *possibility* of him being on the flight. She did not actually tell her mother it was a *certainty*. The situation is *more complicated* than she thought, she says. In fact, Peter might not be home for *some days*. She has travelled up to Birmingham from London, she says, but she cannot stay. There will be a post-mortem, Lisa says. Peter died in an area with many *junkies*. It was a week after he died before he was identified. And it seemed there would be at least one week, possibly two, before he can come home. There

79

may well be two post-mortems, if they charge anyone with his death.

In the meantime, his remains congeal in the drawer of a mortuary in a foreign land. And while his
body is there, the family has gathered here to bury
their child. Outside, the men of the family sit around
the fire keeping a vigil while they argue over whether
Motor Action or Caps United deserves to top the
national soccer league. There is no hope for
Dynamos under its present management, they agree.
Inside the house, the women sing of the transient
nature of our earthly presence. '*Hatina musha panyi-
ka*,' they sing as they wait to see Peter in his coffin
before they can undam the full outpouring of their
grief. They cannot mourn him fully without seeing
his body. He came from the dust and to dust he must
return to be interred whole, intact. They are all here,
my grandfather's brother, my father's nephews and
nieces, the agnatic aunts and uncles as well as the
aunts and uncles by marriage. They continue to
arrive, preparing their faces to meet the faces that
they will meet, composing their faces to masks of
mourning as soon as they glimpse the gates to our
house. They let go then, wailing at the top of their
voices, falling into each other's arms as they stagger
in little dances of grief. Then the moment of emotion over, they ask after one another's health and that

of their families, and their thoughts turn to food.

And in this matter of food lies our anguish.

We cannot feed them all if they continue to pour out like this, and if we must host them for an unknown number of days. We cannot be sure how long it will take to bring Peter home. The small pile of *chema* funeral donations in a bowl on the kitchen table, grubby notes laced with the sweat of many hands, is barely enough to pay for three days' supply of black market milk and bread and sugar. Already the relatives on the paternal side who have the authority to command the daughters-in-law march into the kitchen and demand to know when the feeding will begin. But how to tell people: please go away, we have not started officially to mourn? They have spent money to get here; the old aunts from Shurugwi have taken out their notes from the old pots in which they keep their money. And then to tell them, please, find more money, go away for now and come back later, wearing your most sorrowful faces.

We cannot issue an invitation to a funeral like it is a wedding.

❧

And even as we cannot bury Peter without our relatives, the relatives bring complications beyond the pressing matter of food. They do not accept our decision to bury Peter here in Harare. They will not listen to Jonathan as he explains how fortunate we are to have a burial site, how we had to bribe a council official and still pay double the market price. They insist that our customs dictate that Peter be buried with my father and other ancestors hundreds of kilometres away in Shurugwi. Great-uncle Matyaya who arrived last night has been the most insistent. He trembled with passion as he grasped the rounded end of his walking stick and thumped it on the floor in emphasis. 'Is it not bad enough that Peter died *mhiri kwemakungwa*, over the oceans where the baleful influence of alien spirits could not be discounted? Never before', he said, 'has a son of Chikwiro been buried away from the land of his ancestors.' Jonathan has reached his limits and has to restrain himself from saying to the fathers of the clan that if they want to bury him in Shurugwi, they have to pay for the bus to ferry the mourners there.

◦

'The only good thing about Father's death', Peter had said in his careless way, 'is that we will not have to put up with his tiresome relations.' We learned soon enough that this prediction was premature. Death does not sever the ties; it binds them ever tighter, for it is in death and its attendant processes that kinship

82

asserts its triumphant claims. He had been loaned to us as husband and father, but in death the clan reclaimed him. They buried him in Shurugwi, where we had to travel for hours on uncertain roads if we wanted to visit his grave. Kinship asserted itself through the funeral rites, in the ceremony to release his spirit, and in the accompanying ceremony of inheritance. His family had even attempted to speak on his behalf. They consulted a diviner who interceded between this world and the next: Father did not rest easy, was his uncompromising verdict. It appeared that the reasons for his discomfort were mainly financial.

'He wants the money that he left behind to be divided between his children and the brothers and sisters of his blood,' *Mai*Lisa pronounced.

But my father's spirit, however restless, could not undo the will that he had written and signed in his own hand. And when the Master of the High Court pronounced this as the final word, the aunts and uncles could only curl their mouths into their noses.

❦

They are here, now, the aunts and uncles. They are determined that we meet the costs of their expectations, but that we bear the burden alone just as we shared my father's inheritance without them.

Jonathan is particularly worried about the fuel. He drives at a moderate speed to conserve it. There are snaking queues at the garages, people sleep in their cars, unsure of the hour the fuel will arrive. The garage attendants are endlessly optimistic, the fuel will arrive if not just now, then some time this week. But the queues only grow longer as the attendants become more hopeful. Jonathan is afraid that we may not have enough to last the week. The garages give priority to funeral parties, but they have become wise to the tricks of conmen who pretend to be part of funeral processions and then sell on the fuel at inflated prices. One man even feigned death, almost suffocating in his coffin to get his precious fluid. The attendants insist on seeing the death certificates of the deceased. We have no death certificate, and we will have none unless Lisa comes through for us.

∽

Lisa is the daughter of our father's sister, she calls me *mainini*, little mother, and she calls Jonathan and Peter her uncles. Her mother takes every opportunity to tell us of her latest success.

'Lisa has bought herself a car.'

'Lisa has moved into a bigger flat.'

'Lisa is flying to America, to Canada, to Italy, to France.'

'She has sent money just today, two hundred and fifty billion dollars she sent, it is only two hundred pounds, just imagine. She insists that I go on a holiday, but I told her, no, my child, not on four teachers' annual salary. I said a new stove is more important. Can you believe that she sent more money, five hundred billion dollars? Just imagine. I will buy a new fridge from Radio Limited.'

But of Lisa herself we see very little. She has only been home once in the four years since she went away. She was here two Christmases ago, resplendent in her plastic hair and tight-fitting clothes. She brought us a tray decorated with the names and faces of the kings and queens of England from William the Conqueror to Elizabeth Windsor, and presented it as though it was the one thing needful in our unravelling lives. She chatted brightly about England in her new accent; she pronounces our city's first letter as *haitch*. The sun was too hot, she complained, and she had only been back for two weeks but goodness, wasn't she becoming dark. 'Oh but everyone here is so dark,' she said.

❧

My aunt and my mother have been locked in a life-long war of attrition, the same war that is fought in households across the country between wives on one side, and the mothers and sisters of their husbands on the other. Between my aunt and my mother, it expressed itself in the up-and-down looks from my aunt as she asked, 'Is that a new dress?' and then, 'I would have thought with *your issues* you would not have time for such finery.' It expressed itself in my mother's finger running across furniture to collect dust, in her fastidious eye that picked out the merest hint of a smear on the windows.

Above all, it expressed itself in the competition between their children. We have not achieved Lisa's material success, having sent no stoves and fridges from Radio Limited home to my mother. But even our modest successes, my soon-to-be-achieved medical degree and Jonathan's accountancy qualification, are cancelled out by Peter's failures.

I often think of my aunt as the opposite of that trio of horsemen galloping though the night to bring the good news from Ghent to Aix in my favourite poem as a child. She crosses the city from Mufakose to Greendale in her eagerness to bring us bad news before anyone else can do so. And for all the distance between London and Birmingham, Lisa seems to be remarkably well informed about Peter's failures. She passes one Peter story after another to her mother who endures the discomfort and oppressive heat of one commuter omnibus after another as she arrives to sweat out her bad news.

Then finally, she brings us the worst news of all.

But we were not to worry, she said.

Lisa would bring Peter home.

❧

As she boasts of Lisa's accomplishments, my aunt chooses not to recall that it was my father who said to her, 'Sister, your daughter has finished her nursing diploma. Instead of rotting in some rural outpost, why does she not try her fortune where others have gone?'

It was my father who gave Lisa the money for her air ticket. My mother did not speak a civil word to my father for a week after his decision to buy Lisa's ticket; their voices rose in the night, my mother insisting that his first duty was to his own children, Father saying that it was in their children's interests that others in the family succeeded so that we all shared the family burdens, and my mother saying that he was too weak for his own good, and did not our elders say that if you rear a dog on milk, it would only end up biting your hand?

❧

Though he did not live to see Lisa's success, he continued to do good for us from beyond the grave. It was his life insurance money that sent Peter to

London. I try to avoid thinking it is not fair, it should have been me, and I would have honoured Father's memory. Even then, I could see the sense of the plan; I had my studies, Jonathan his training. And there was Peter, shiftless and idle. Harare was not the place for a nineteen-year-old boy who was bright and able, but too lazy to achieve the grades to get into the local universities, and who could not get a job but liked to drink.

So we sent him to London.

He had been more fortunate than those of our countrymen and women who have flooded England to wipe old people's bottoms for a living. No menial labour for Mother's last-born son. Father's money had paid his tuition. But Peter's ambitions were as broad as the range of courses available to him; he moved from architecture to business studies, from economics to statistics, from quantity surveying to computer science. 'This time, I won't change my mind,' he said every time that he changed his mind.

∾

Wafa wanaka, our elders say. Not only does this mean that death is the ultimate peace, it also means that we are not to speak ill of the dead. Once a person has crossed over to the realm of the spirits, he takes his transgressions with him, and we speak only of the good. So as we mourn Peter, we are to forget how he bled the family dry. It was not enough that my mother paid his fees and provided his accommodation and his food. The phone would ring, shrill and insistent at three in the morning. I would stumble to answer it, banging my foot in the darkness as there was never electricity at night, I would rush for the phone hoping to get to it before my mother picked up the extension in her bedroom, I would grab for it too late, to hear my mother answer as Peter said with no ceremony, 'I need money.'

'*Nhai* Peter,' my mother would plead. 'What hour is this to be calling and asking for money? How can you say you need money, what about all the money we have sent?'

'I need money.'

This was Peter, who always got his way, who picked out the biggest apple, the brightest-coloured kite. And as she had done all his life, my mother gave in. She bought pounds on the black market and smuggled them to him, risking a jail term under the newly enacted crime of externalising foreign currency. And we had no jam on our bread, no milk in our tea while Peter drank away our father's inheritance in London.

Wafa wanaka; we are to forget that before he went to England, Peter stole anything he could from the family, including the stethoscope that Father left me, the stethoscope through which I heard the sound of my heart as a child, sitting on Father's knee as he teased me and said there was a laughing sound from my left ventricular cavity and a crying sound from my right ventricular cavity, and I should always listen to the left side for in this matter left was right; the stethoscope that was engraved 'Peter Munyaradzi Chikwiro: Best Results University of Aberdeen Medical School, 1972', the stethoscope that I hoped to use to listen to the heartbeats of my own patients.

Wafa wanaka; we are to forget the increasingly hysterical phone calls as Peter threatened to take his own life if Mother did not send more money, the phone calls that led her to sell all the shares that Father had left to provide her security, to take out a loan at eight hundred per cent interest, a loan she struggled to repay from her modest teacher's salary that became a trifle as inflation rose first from thirty to seventy per cent, then from one hundred and seventeen to nine hundred and sixty-seven point five three per cent until it broke the one thousand per cent barrier. We are to forget that my mother's blood pressure rose with inflation as she sold item after item to feed the demands from England, her visits to the doctor becoming more frequent as she sought to control Peter's excesses from seven thousand kilometres, until he said again he would kill himself if she did not send money, and my mother, broken by approaching penury, fatigue and illness, said, 'Then do, Peter. Do, for maybe then we will all get some rest.'

❧

There is laughter from the back garden as the daughters-in-law cook over an open fire. 'You are not serious,' says Mukai. 'That cannot be what she said.'

'Honestly!' says a voice that I recognise as my Uncle Donald's wife. 'I swear by my father who is buried at Serima Mission that that is exactly what she said.'

There is more laughter. It is not out of place in this house of mourning. This is how things are; we meet only to bury our dead. And why not laugh as we do so? We part only to meet again at funerals. The statisticians whose business it is to quantify, measure and average human experience say that there are three thousand deaths every month in our country, and I imagine that in this very month there are three thousand homes holding three thousand wakes, there are three thousand lots of *chema* funeral donations, three thousand homes in which will arise the sudden quarrels between those who do not like each other but must surrender to the undeniable imperative of

91

blood, three thousands lots of daughters-in-law laughing over the funeral pots.

As I turn away from the laughter, I am followed by Uncle Donald's wife who pulls me into a corner and tells me that *Mai*Lisa has been *saying things*. I am as used to *Mai*Lisa saying things as I am to the solicitous relatives who ensure that we hear every word.

'I do not mean to be a gossip,' she says, in what she considers a whisper, 'but *Mai*Lisa is saying your family is pestering her daughter, and that it is not her fault Peter drank away his father's inheritance, and what sort of education did you and Jonathan receive if it means that you must rely on her child, and anyway, she has told Lisa to do what is best for herself, to do what is convenient to her and not worry about what ungrateful people might think. For, do not the elders say that if you rear a dog on milk, it will bite your hand the next morning?'

'You know I am not one to gossip,' Uncle Donald's wife says again, 'but I feel that your mother should be told these things.'

My mother would not care if *Mai*Lisa spewed out her poison before her. She has turned her face to the wall and does not always respond to Mukai's entreaties to eat or to rest, or to walk in the garden. She no longer asks after the news from England. I know that she must think of the words that were spoken between her and Peter, and that she must wake in her living nightmare of having said words that cannot be taken back; words that were spoken out of defeat and exhaustion; words that mean everything and nothing.

I am the only one apart from Peter who heard those words, but I cannot comfort her. I cannot say to her: 'It was not you. This was a path he was on from which we could not divert him.' To say these platitudes would be to acknowledge that those words were said, to acknowledge that they were said would mean asking questions that only Peter can answer. So I find myself hoping for the only thing that can make it better, that the post-mortem will show that he did not die of his own hand, that another murdered my brother.

∾

As the days become nights and the weeks become one month, Jonathan and I resolve to handle the matter ourselves. We go to the British embassy to apply for visas to go to England. Inside we are caught in a sea of humanity whose hopes are pinned on those words: 'Leave to enter granted.' As we wait, my attention is attracted by a woman in a red beret who has her eyes closed as her lips move in prayer.

I am close enough to hear her mutter, 'Lord you are

mighty, Jehovah. Look on your suffering servant and assist her, Jehovah. I call upon your blessings this day, Almighty.' She has to interrupt her prayer as her number is called. Her shouted 'Thank you, Jehovah' as she sees the magic words in her passport is infectious, people crowd around her to see and marvel at the visa, to touch the passport, and maybe transfer some of her good fortune onto themselves. Her joy suggests that she is not just a tourist exulting at the thought of seeing the changing of the guard at Buckingham Palace.

This is the only light moment that morning. The window is shut as Jonathan and I get to it, and we have to stand in another queue. We are served by a man who does not look us in the face, but ticks our forms as he eyes his watch.

'What is your business in England?'

'One of us must go to England to bring my dead brother home.'

'Do you have his death certificate?'

'No, sir, we do not. We need to go there to get it.'

He looks up at that. 'Then this could be just a story you are telling me. How do I know you really have a dead brother if you do not show me his death certificate?'

Jonathan struggles to explain. 'The death certificate cannot be issued without a post-mortem. And that is taking too long.'

And I say to myself, Jonathan does not explain properly, he must explain that only when they have separated his brain from the cerebral cavity, separated the *medulla oblongata* from the frontal lobe, done toxicological tests, only then will they determine what killed him, only then will they be able to say whether he died by his own hand or by that of another. Tell him about the relatives, I will him. They will not go until Peter comes home. Tell them about the body viewing. How can we have a funeral without a body to view, without people filing by to pay respects as he lies in his coffin in our living room, all the while the daughters-in-law singing him away?

I open my mouth to voice these thoughts but the man is impatient, and waves us off. As Jonathan continues to plead, the official is joined by a woman who has been hovering in the background. She has heard only a part of the conversation, and grabs the end of what she thinks she has heard. In her crisp English voice, she says: 'If you want to see your brother, just ask him for an invitation letter. We must see his bank statements over the last three months, his lease agreement, and proof of immigration status. It is all there in the Guidance Note.'

'But he is dead!' I cry out at last. 'We want to bring him home because he is dead.'

The others in the room cannot pretend not to have heard. They turn their faces away as if afraid that our misfortune will infect them. The woman's face reddens and she hides her embarrassment behind the mask of officialdom. 'Well, in that case, we have to see the death certificate.'

Our consolation must be that even if they give us the visas, we cannot afford the flight. Jonathan had said he would borrow the money, but the air ticket alone is more than his annual salary.

❧

And so we continue to rely on Lisa. I do not always get through to London. I sit for hours sometimes while the mechanical voice from the exchange tells me that calls to my destination are not possible at this time. When I do get through, the calls are not always answered, and when they are, Lisa can barely control her impatience.

'*Maininika*,' she says. 'I cannot do more than I am doing already. Should I break into the mortuary and steal his body? Or is it that I am to turn myself into Peter *wacho* so that you can bury me?'

I resolve then that I will pay back every pound that she has spent if it takes me my entire life.

❧

We dance our dance of sorrow as the daughters-in-law keen for the new arrivals. I am a stranger in my own home, surrounded by women who wear my clothes without asking, emptying my bowels by candlelight in the middle of the night for it is only then that I can be private without someone banging on the door, asking, 'Who is there?' and then saying, 'Ah, is it you, Mary, how long do you think you will be?'

Just when I think that I cannot take any more, the phone call comes that promises that this time Peter really will be on the Friday morning flight. *Mai*Lisa takes it upon herself to call back those relatives that had left. She insists that she come with us, for is it not her child who has made the arrangements? And anyway, she says, my mother is not in a fit state to go. But my mother insists on going with us and we cannot refuse her.

We make our way to the airport as we have done before, and wait with others as we have done before. The scenes are the same as the last time we were here, happy relations waiting for something nice from London. Jonathan doubts that Lisa really will come. So we expect Peter to be unaccompanied, and Jonathan identifies himself to the airline. *Mai*Lisa adds to the tension of the wait by mistaking every young woman of Lisa's build for her daughter.

'There she is, I see her, Lisa, Lisa, psst, here, Lisa',

only to have her waving arm fall to her side as she says, 'Ahh, honestly, this is what old age does. I need glasses, surely. Ahh, there she is, Lisa, psst.'

But there is no Lisa among the passengers. Jonathan checks again with the airline, but there is nothing for us. He cannot find the words to tell us, and he only shakes his head. My mother begins to laugh, a sound that is worse than any crying.

*Mai*Lisa stands aside and studies the contents of a curio shop through the glass windows. All the while, I can see her stealing glances at my mother. As I watch her pretending interest in a zebra-skin rug, I feel rage so bitter that it is like bile in my mouth. I am unaware of the first hot tears that course down my cheeks. They are the first tears that I have shed, but I do not cry for him, they are tears of hatred for him and his miserable little life and what he has done to our family.

My mother's moment of hysteria does not last and it gives way to her usual catatonia. She lets Jonathan and Mukai lead her away. *Mai*Lisa pants after us. 'Not to worry,' she says, 'she will be on the next flight. The next flight, definitely.' She mumbles theories that no one wants to hear. I try to shut out her voice, and concentrate so hard that I do not hear my name being called. A hand on my shoulder brings me back from myself. It is a woman in the faded green and beige livery of the national airline.

'You are surely Mary Chikwiro,' she says. 'I have a picture of you here.' Through my tears I see a picture of me with Lisa and Peter sitting beneath the mango tree outside our house, weeks before Lisa left for England. The woman smiles again and says, 'I have something from your cousin Lisa. She said it was a special delivery, and didn't want to have to go through customs.'

I blink away my tears but she is oblivious to my distress.

'People send me with things, you know, nice things from London. I charge only fifty pounds per package. It's a living, isn't?'

She now seems to notice my mood and says quickly, 'Here is the package. Enjoy.' She smiles uncertainly as she thrusts the package into my arms.

I take the box and walk towards Jonathan who stands some metres apart from the women. We both look at the package wrapped in gaudy purple and silver paper and tied with purple ribbon. I open the box to reveal an urn of dark wood. Peter's name is engraved on a brass plate on the lid. There is nothing to say. We follow my mother and *Mai*Lisa out to the car park.

∾ In the Heart of the Golden Triangle ∾

You hear your mother say to *Mai*Mufundisi that her daughter has a big, big house deep in the golden triangle. 'Right in the heart of the golden triangle,' you hear her say. In the golden triangle, you live a stone's throw from the Governor of the Central Bank. In the street behind the French Ambassador's residence, your house is next to the residence of the British High Commissioner. You try to remember that you are to call him the British Ambassador now, because your President pulled your country out of the Commonwealth.

Your maid brings you morning tea in bed. She says she did this with the British High Commissioner's wife, remember to call him Ambassador. You drink your tea at leisure because you do not have to work. Your husband is the Director in the Treasury Department of a Big Merchant Bank. 'We have branches all over Africa,' their adverts say, 'but our roots are here in Zimbabwe.'

You call your maid Joyce and she calls you Madam. You don't admit this to anyone, even to yourself, but you employed her only because she worked for the British High Commissioner remember to call him the British Ambassador before he was asked to leave the country for stating the obvious in a country where the truth can be spoken only in the private chambers of the mind.

'She makes flaky puff pastry that is as light as a feather,' you say to your friends as you drink afternoon tea. They complain about their maids, and you listen and chime in with stories of maids that you have employed, maids that you have sacked and maids that have stolen from you.

'Maidei stole my Ferragamo shoes,' you say. This happened five years ago, but the incident still rankles. Joyce is not Maidei, she is coming along nicely, you think, you *hope* because you could not bear to go through another maid; you have been through thirty-five. After you drink the morning tea that she brings you, you get up, but you may as well lie in because in the golden triangle there are never enough things to do.

You spend the day looking for ways to fill in the hours, to stretch them out so that they run into each other. There are brunches and lunches, and teas, and dinners. You have eaten through the menu at Amanzi and Imba Matombo. There are tombolas and cake-bakes and bring-and-buys. There are concerts at your son's school.

Your son was in the same class as the President's son, before the President complained about the fees and withdrew his son to be home-schooled. Your son goes to a school that was too expensive for the President. It gives you a thrill, just to think about it.

You leave the house, alternating your BMW with your Range Rover. The security guard whose name you can never remember almost breaks his leg as he runs to stand by the gate which does not need to be opened because it is automatic and electric. He salutes you as you drive out. You head out to the school to listen to your son play the piano. He misses most of the notes. Mrs Robinson, the music teacher from England, sits with a tight smile on her face, but you don't notice it. You drive with your son to Sam Levy's. You talk on your phone while he bullies other children off the jumping castle.

And you think, *Maybe I should do some shopping.*

There is very little shopping in the golden triangle. You buy your milk and bread at Honeydew. In the supermarket, every month, you buy three hampers in bright colours, hampers carefully chosen to approximate the basic needs of your maid, gardener and security guard: Perfection soap and coarse maize meal, cooking oil and dry beans, corned beef ground from the unmentionable parts of the cow, dried *matemba* fish that taste of nothing but fish bones and brains, Lifebuoy soap.

There is nothing in the shops for you.

When you want to shop, you fly out, out of the triangle and up, up on the wings of freedom, on South African Airways you travel together with the wives of Cabinet ministers who do all their grocery shopping in Johannesburg, even as their husbands promise to end food shortages. There you buy your proudly South African products in Rosebank and Sandton because as you said to your friend Bertha last year, Eastgate has become just too cheap. You sat behind the First Lady on your last flight.

She flipped through *True Love* magazine.

Your eyes met as you passed to take your seat.

You did not like her eye make-up.

∾

In the golden triangle your children speak only English, English sentences that all begin 'Mummy I want . . .', 'Mummy can you buy me . . .', 'Mummy where is daddy?' Daddy is often not there, he is out doing the deals and playing the golf that ensures that you continue to live in the golden triangle. You say this to the children, but your son is old enough to know that golf is not played in the pitch blackness of the night. You stop his questions with a shout. He turns and locks himself in his room.

You breathe out your remorse at yelling at your son but you cannot tell him the truth. That you share your husband with another woman.

Imbadiki, she is called. That is not her real name; that only means she inhabits the small house while you live in the big one in the heart of the golden triangle. Her name is Sophia. She is twenty-five years younger than your husband. You know this because you had your husband followed. Not that he even tried to hide it. No man can be expected to be faithful, he has said often enough. It is not nature's intention. He said the same thing to you when you met in secret away from the eyes of his first wife.

And as you gasped beneath him, above him and beside him, as he put his hands on your haunches and drew you to him, you agreed, no man could be expected to be faithful, yes, you said, oh yes, you said, just like that, you said, right there. You are fifteen years younger than he is, and his wife before you was five years younger than he was. You go to the gym, where you have a girl who plucks the hair out of your eyebrows, and the hair from under your arms, and the hair from your pubis. You pay someone to scrub your feet and to pummel you with hot stones.

The small house cannot become the big house.

You worry because you have not found condoms in his pockets. You find yourself hoping that he keeps them in the small house. You watch for the tell-tale signs of illness which crosses over into the golden triangle and touches your gardener Timothy and your security guard whose name you can never remember. They both have the red lips that speak their status. The only red lips you want are from lipstick but you fear that you may have them too if your husband continues to establish small houses all over the city.

You have parties in the golden triangle, where men braai meat and talk about business while you sit with other women and talk about, you are not really sure what you talk about. You see your friends at these parties, Laetitia, who used to be a teacher before she married a banker. Tendai, who used to be a model before she married a banker. Bertha who used to be a secretary before she married a banker. You talk about your old friend Norma who used to be the small house of a banker before she married him, and who was evicted from the golden triangle, and now lives in a house in Ashdown Park that has a yard of only a quarter of an acre.

'*Akadhingurwa* Norma,' you laugh about it when you are drunk with your friends and Oliver

Mtukudzi is playing on the stereo. In all the malice of your *Schadenfreude*, you make it all about her, she was getting full of herself, Norma, you all agree. Away from your friends, the ice grips your heart and you work out twice as long at the gym to keep Norma's fate from your door.

You watch Timothy plant birds of paradise in the narrow space between the lawn and the driveway. You imagine the driveway lined with the flowers, driving through four hundred metres of birds of paradise, driving past their purple and orange plumes. You have the sudden urge to scream, but you don't know why, all you know is that no one can hear if you scream behind your walls; your echoes will be absorbed in the verdancy of your garden, in the garden furniture that you imported from Italy. Your scream will bounce off your Jackson Munyeza tennis court to ripple silently in your Jackson Munyeza swimming pool.

You see yourself at sixteen, always you go back to how you were at sixteen, surrounded by other schoolgirls in a world where achievement was everything. Who gets best marks, who can run the fastest, who can come up with the best tricks to plague the nuns. You were happy to see an old school friend the other day, and you fell into each other's arms. Your voices rang out as you cried out in happy reminiscence.

Do you remember, do you remember?

She turned to your children and said, 'Your mother was a really good discus thrower,' and she turned to you and said it was nice to see you Catherine, and you did not tell her that your name was not Catherine, she had confused you with someone else because you did not throw the discus at all.

'It was the javelin,' you say to yourself at the traffic lights. It is all you can do to stop yourself crying. 'It was the javelin.' High, high, flew the javelin, higher, always higher. The cars behind you honk. Moments later, you turn into Glenara. You drive over three potholes, one after the other, but in the cushioned comfort of your four-by-four, you don't feel a thing.

∾ The Mupandawana Dancing Champion ∾

When the prices of everything went up ninety-seven times in one year, M'dhara Vitalis Mukaro came out of retirement to make the coffins in which we buried our dead. In a space of only six months, he became famous twice over, as the best coffin maker in the district and as the Mupandawana Dancing Champion.

Fame is an elastic concept, especially in a place like this, where we all know the smells of each other's armpits. Mupandawana, full name Gutu-Mupanda-wana Growth Point, is bigger than a village but it is not yet a town. I have become convinced that the government calls Mupandawana a growth point merely to divert us from the reality of our present squalor with optimistic predictions about our booming future. As it is not even a townlet, a townling, or half a fraction of a town, there was much rejoicing at a recent groundbreaking ceremony for a new row of

Blair toilets when the District Commissioner shared with us his vision for town status for Mupandawana by the year 2065. Ours is one of the biggest growth points in the country, but the only real growth is in the number of people waiting to buy coffins, and the lengthening line of youngsters waiting to board the Wabuda Wanatsa buses blasting Chimbetu songs all the way to Harare.

You will not find me joining that queue out of Mupandawana. When the Ministry despatched me here to teach at the local secondary, I was relieved to escape the headaches of Harare with its grasping women who will not let go until your wallet is empty. Mupandawana is the perfect place from which to study life, which appears to me to be no more than the punchline to a cosmic joke played by a particularly mordant being.

So I observe life, and teach geography to school-children whose only interest in my subject is knowledge of the exact distance between Mupandawana and London, Mupandawana and Johannesburg, Mupandawana and Gaborone, Mupandawana and Harare. If I cared enough, I would tell them that there is nothing there to rush for, *kumhunga hakuna ipwa*, as my late mother used to say.

But let them go, they shall find out soon enough.

Mine is not a lonely life. In those moments when

solitude quarrels with me, I enjoy the company of my two friends, Jeremiah, who teaches agriculture, and Bobojani who goes where Jeremiah goes. And then there are the Growth Pointers, as I call them, the people of Mupandawana whose lives prove my theory that life is one big jest at the expense of humanity.

Take M'dhara Vitalis, the coffin maker.

Before he retired, he worked in a furniture factory in Harare. He had been trained in the old days, M'dhara Vitalis told us on the first occasion Jeremiah, Bobojani and I drank with him. 'If the leg of one of my chairs had got you in the head, *vapfanha*, you would have woken up to tell your story in heaven,' he said. 'The President sits in one of my chairs. Real oak, *vapfanha*. I made furniture from oak, teak, mahogany, cedar, ash *chaiyo*, even Oregon pine. Not these *zhing-zhong* products from China. They may look nice and flashy but they will crack in a minute.'

On this mention of China, Bobo made a joke about the country becoming Zhim-Zhim-Zhimbabwe because the ruling party had sold the country to the Chinese. Not to be outdone, Jeremiah said, 'A group of Zanu PF supporters arrives at the pearly gates. Saint Peter is greatly shocked, and goes to consult God. God says, but ruling party supporters are also my children. Saint Peter goes to fetch them, but rushes back alone shouting they've gone, they've gone. How can the ruling party supporters just disappear, says God. I am talking about the pearly gates, says Peter.'

We laughed, keeping our voices low because the District Commissioner was seated in the corner below the window.

∾

M'dhara Vitalis had looked forward to setting down the tools of his trade and retiring to answer the call of the land. 'You don't know how lucky you are,' he was often heard to say to the fellows who idled around Mupandawana. 'You have no jobs so you can plough your fields.'

He had spent so much time in Harare that he appeared not to see that the rows to be ploughed were stony; when the rains came, there was no seed, and when there was seed, there were no rains. Even those like Jeremiah who liked farming so much so that they had swallowed books all the way to the agricultural college at Chibhero had turned their backs on the land, in Jeremiah's case, by choosing to teach the theory of farming to children who, given even an eighth of a chance, would sooner choose the lowliest messenger jobs in the cities than a life of tilling the land.

M'dhara Vitalis was forced to retire three years earlier than anticipated. His employer told him that the company was shutting down because they could not afford the foreign currency. There would not be money for a pension, he was told, the money had been invested in a bank whose directors had run off with it *kwazvakarehwa* to England. He had been allowed to keep his overalls, and had been given some of the tools that he had used in the factory. And because the owner was also closing down another factory, one that manufactured shoes, M'dhara Vitalis and all the other employees were each given three pairs of shoes.

Jeremiah, Bobo and I saw him as he got off the Wabuda Wanatsa bus from Harare. 'Thirty years, *vakomana*,' he said to us, as he shook his head. 'You work thirty years for one company and this is what you get. *Shuwa, shuwa*, pension *yebhutsu. Heh?* Shoes, instead of a pension. Shoes. These, these . . .'

The words caught in his throat.

'*Ende futi dzinoshinya*, all the pairs are half a size too small for me,' he added when he had recovered his voice. We commiserated with him as best we could. We poured out all the feeling contained in our hearts.

'Sorry, M'dhara,' I said.

'Rough, M'dhara,' said Jeremiah.

'Tight,' said Bobojani.

We watched him walk off carefully in his snug-fitting shoes, the plastic bag with the other two pairs dangling from his left hand.

117

'Pension *yebhutsu*,' Jeremiah said, and, even as we pitied him, we laughed until tears ran down Jeremiah's cheeks and we had to pick Bobojani off the ground.

For all that he did not have a real pension, M'dhara Vitalis was happy to retire. Some three kilometres from the growth point was the homestead that he had built with money earned from the factory, with three fields for shifting cultivation. Between them, he and his wife managed well enough, somehow making do until the drought came in two consecutive years and inflation zoomed and soared and spun the roof off the country. M'dhara Vitalis went back to Harare to look for another job, but who wanted an old man like him when there were millions unemployed? He looked around Mupandawana and was fortunate to find work making coffins. M'dhara Vitalis was so efficient that he made a small contribution to the country's rising unemployment – his employer found it convenient to fire two other carpenters. And that was how he became known as the coffin maker with the nimblest fingers this side of the Great Dyke.

∽

We had seen his hands at work, but of his nimble feet and his acrobatics on the dance floors of Harare, we had only heard. As the person who told us these stories was the man himself, there was reason to believe that he spoke as one who ululated in his own praise. As Jeremiah said, 'There is too much seasoning in M'dhara Vita's stories.'

All his exploits seemed to have taken place in the full glare of the public light. 'I danced at Copacabana, Job's Night Spot and the Aquatic Complex. There is one night I will never forget when I danced at Mushandirapamwe and the floor cleared of dancers. All that the people could do was to stand and watch. *Vakamira ho-o*,' he told us. We laughed into our beers, Jeremiah, Bobojani and I, but, as we soon came to see, we laughed too much and we laughed too soon.

M'dhara Vita's employer was the Member of Parliament for our area. As befitting such a man of the people, the Honourable had a stake in the two most thriving enterprises in the growth point, so that the profits from Kurwiragono Investments t/a No Matter Funeral Parlour and Coffin Suppliers accumulated interest in the same bank account as those from Kurwiragono Investments t/a Why Leave Guesthouse and Disco-Bar. And being one on whom fortune had smiled, our Honourable could naturally not confine his prosperous seed to only one woman. Why Leave was managed by Felicitas, the Honourable's fourth wife, a generous sort who had done her bit to make a good number of men happy before she settled into relative domesticity with the Honourable. As one of those happy men, I retained very fond memories of her, and often stepped into the Guesthouse for a drink and to pass the time. She always had an eye out for the next chance, Felicitas, which is how she came to replace me with the Honourable, and she decided that what the bar needed was a dancing competition.

The first I knew of it was not from Felicitas herself, but when I saw groups of dust-covered schoolchildren at break time dancing the *kongonya*. Now, the sexually suggestive *kongonya* is the dance of choice at ruling party gatherings, so that I thought that they must be practising for a visit from yet another dignitary. Later that evening as I passed the Guesthouse I saw another crowd of children dancing the *kongonya*, while another pointed to the wall of the building. Intrigued by this random outbreak of *kongonya* in the youth of Mupandawana, I approached the Guesthouse. The youngsters scattered on my approach, and I saw that they had been admiring a poster on which was portrayed the silhouette outline of a couple captured in mid-dance. The man's back was bent so far that his head almost touched the ground, while his female partner, of a voluptuousness that put me in mind of Felicitas, had her hands on her knees with her bottom almost touching the ground.

120

Below this enraptured couple were the words:

Why Leave Guesthouse and Disco-Bar in association with Mupandawana District Development Council is proud to present the search for the:

Mupandawana
Dancing
Champion

Join us for a night of celebration and dancing!
One Night Only!!

Details followed of the competition to be held a fortnight from then, and the main prizes to be won, the most notable of which was one drink on the house once a week for three months.

Mupandawana is a place of few new public pleasures. In the following two weeks, the excitement escalated and reached a pitch on the night itself. In their cheap and cheerful clothes, Mupandawana's highest and lowest gathered in the main room of the Why Leave Guesthouse and poured out into the night: the lone doctor doing penance at the district hospital, the nurses, the teachers, the security guards, the storekeeper from Chawawanaidyanehama Cash and Carry and his two giggling girl assistants, the District Commissioner in all his frowning majesty, the policemen from the camp, a few soldiers, the people from the nearby and outlying villages.

Tapping feet and impatient twitches and shakes showed that the people were itching to get started, and when Felicitas turned on the music, they needed no further encouragement. The music thumped into the room, the Bhundu Boys, Alick Macheso and the Orchestra Mberikwazvo, Andy Brown and Storm, System Tazvida and the Chazezesa Challengers, Cephas 'Motomuzhinji' Mashakada and Muddy Face, Hosiah Chipanga and Broadway Sounds, Mai Charamba and the Fishers of Men, Simon 'Chopper' Chimbetu and the Orchestra Dendera Kings, Tongai 'Dehwa' Moyo and Utakataka Express, and, as no occasion could be complete without him, Oliver 'Tuku' Mtukudzi and the Black Spirits. They sang out their celebratory anthems of life gone right; they sang out their woeful, but still danceable, laments of things gone wrong. And to all these danced the Growth Pointers, policeman and teacher, nurse and villager, man and woman, young and old. There was *kongonya*, more *kongonya*, and naturally more *kongonya* – ruling party supporters in Mupandawana are spread as thickly as the rust on the ancient Peugeot 504 that the Honourable's son crashed and abandoned at Sadza Growth Point. Bobojani was in there with the best of them, shuffling a foot away from the District Commissioner, while Jeremiah and I watched from the bar.

The Growth Pointers did themselves proud. The security guard who stood watch outside the Building Society danced the Borrowdale even better than Alick Macheso. Dzinganisayi, widely considered to be the Secretary-General of the Mupandawana branch of ZATO (aka the Zimbabwe Association of Thieves' Organisations) proved to be as talented on the dance floor as he was in making both attended and unattended objects vanish. Nyengeterayi from Chawawanaidyanehama Cash and Carry got down on hands and knees and improvised a dance that endangered her fingers, given the stomping, dancing feet around her.

And who knew that the new fashion and fabrics teacher could move her hips like that? As I watched her gyrate to Tuku, a stirring arose in my loins, and I began to reconsider the benefits of long-term companionship.

Then, out of the corner of my eye, I saw M'dhara Vita enter the room.

He was dressed in a suit that declared its vintage as circa 1970s. The trouser legs were flared, while the beltline that must have once hugged his hips and waist was rolled up and tied around his waistline with an old tie. The jacket had two vents at the back. He wore a bright green shirt with the collar covering that of his jacket. On his head was a hat of the kind

123

worn by men of his age, but his was set at a rakish angle, almost covering one eye. And on his feet were one-third of his pension.

'*Ko*, Michael Jackson*ka*,' Jeremiah said as we nudged each other.

M'dhara Vitalis gave us a casual nod as, showing no signs of painful feet, he walked slowly to the dance floor.

And then he danced.

The security guard's Borrowdale became a Mbaresdale. Dzinganisayi's movements proved to be those of a rank amateur. Nyengeterayi's innovations were revealed to be no more than the shallow ambitions of callow youth. M'dhara Vitalis danced them off the floor to the sidelines where they stood to watch with the rest of us. He knew all the latest dances, and the oldest too. We gaped at his reebok and his water pump. He stunned us with his running man. He killed us with his robot. And his snake dance and his break-dance made us stand and say *ho-o*. His moonwalk would have made Michael himself stand and say *ho-o*. The floor cleared, until only he and the fashion and fabrics teacher were dancing.

M'dhara Vitalis was here. The teacher was there.

The teacher was here. M'dhara Vitalis was there.

M'dhara Vitalis moved his hips. The teacher moved her waist.

M'dhara Vitalis moved his neck and head.

The teacher did a complicated twirl with her arms.

M'dhara Vitalis did some fancy footwork, *mapantsula* style.

The teacher lifted her right leg off the ground and shook her right buttock.

And then Felicitas put on Chamunorwa Nebeta and the Glare Express. As the first strains of *Tambai Mese Mujairirane* filled the room, we saw M'dhara Vitalis transformed. He wriggled his hips. He closed his eyes and whistled. He turned his back to us and used the vent in the back of the jacket to expose his bottom as he said, '*Pesu, pesu,*' moving the jacket first to one side and then to the other.

'Watch that waist,' I said to Jeremiah.

'*Chovha George!*' said the District Commissioner.

'If only I was a woman,' said Jeremiah.

That last dance sealed it, the fashion and fabrics teacher conceded the floor. By popular acclaim, M'dhara Vita was crowned Mupandawana Dancing Champion. It was a night that Mupandawana would not forget.

~

This was just as well because the one-night-only threat of the poster came true in a way that Felicitas had not anticipated. Two days after M'dhara Vita's triumph, the Governor of our province summoned our Honourable MP to his office in Masvingo. A bright young spark, one of the countless army of men who are paid to get offended on behalf of the ruling party, had taken a careful look at the poster and noticed that the first letters of the words Mupandawana Dancing Champion spelled out the acronym of the opposition party, the unmentionable Movement for Democratic Change. Naturally, this had to be conveyed to the appropriate channels.

'What business does a ruling party MP have in promoting the opposition, the puppets, those led by tea boys, the detractors who do not understand that the land is the economy and the economy is the land and that the country will never be a colony again, those who seek to reverse the consolidation of the gains of our liberation struggle,' so said the Governor, shaking with rage. I only knew that he shook with rage because Felicitas said he did, and she only knew because the Honourable told her so.

The upshot of this was that there were no more dance competitions, and M'dhara Vita the coffin maker remained the undefeated dancing champion of our growth point. He took his a one-drink-a-week prize for what it was worth, insisting on a half-bottle of undiluted Château brandy every Friday evening. 'Why can't he drink Chibuku like a normal man his age?' Felicitas asked, with rather bad grace, to which I responded that if he had been a normal man of his age, he would not have been the dancer he was.

To appreciate his skill is to understand that he was an old man. They had no birth certificates in the days when he was born, or at least none for people born in the rural areas, so that when he trained as a carpenter at Bondolfi and needed a pass to work in the towns, his mother had estimated his age by trying to recall how old he was when the mission school four kilometres from his village had been built. As befitting one who followed in the professional footsteps of the world's most famous carpenter, he had chosen 25 December as his birthday, so that his age was a random selection and he could well have been older than his official years. What was beyond dispute was that he danced in defiance of the wrinkles around his eyes.

Even if he had not got his drinks on the house, many of us would have bought him, if not his favourite brandy, then a less expensive alternative. There were no competitions and no more posters, but we began to gather at the Guesthouse every Friday evening to watch M'dhara Vita. Fuelled on by the bottom-of-the-barrel brandy and the *museve* music, his gymnastics added colour to our grey Fridays.

It was no different on that last Friday.

'Boys, boys,' he said as he approached the bar where I stood with Bobojani, Jeremiah and a group of other drinkers.

'*Ndeipi* M'dhara,' Jeremiah greeted him in the casual way that we talked to him; none of that respect-for-the-elders routine with M'dhara Vita. He cracked a joke at our expense, and we gave it right back to him, he knocked back his drink, and proceeded to the dance floor. Felicitas had come to understand that it was the Congolese rumba that demanded agile waists and rubber legs that really got him moving. So on that night, the Lumumbashi Stars blasted out of the stereo as M'dhara Vitalis took centre stage. He stood a while, as though to let the brandy and the music move its way though his ears and mouth to his brain and pelvis. Then he ground his hips in time to the rumba, all the while his eyes closed, and his arms stretched out in front of him.

'*Ichi chimudhara chirambakusakara,*' whistled Jeremiah, echoing the generally held view that M'dhara Vitalis was in possession of a secret elixir of youth.

'I am Vitalis, shortcut Vita, *ilizwo lami ngi*Vitalis, danger *basopo. Waya waya waya waya!*' He got down to the ground, rolled and shook. We crowded around him, relishing this new dance that we had not seen before. He twitched to the right, and to the left. The music was loud as we egged him on. He convulsed in response to our cheering. His face shone, and he looked to us as if to say, 'Clap harder.'

And we did.

It was only when the song ended and we gave him a rousing ovation and still he did not get up that we realised that he would never get up, and that he had not been dancing, but dying.

❧

As M'dhara Vitalis left Why Leave feet first, it was up to Bobojani, with his usual eloquence, to provide a fitting commentary on the evening's unexpected event.

'Tight,' he said.

There was not much to add after that.

We buried him in one of the last coffins he ever made. I don't know whether he would have appreciated that particular irony. I am sure, though, that he would have appreciated making the front page of the one and only national daily newspaper.

The story of his death appeared right under the daily picture of the President. If you folded the newspaper three-quarters of the way to hide the story in which was made the sunny prediction that inflation was set to go down to two million, seven hundred

129

and fifty-seven per cent by year end, all you saw was the story about M'dhara Vita. They wrote his name as Fidelis instead of Vitalis, and called him a pensioner when he hadn't got a pension; unless, of course, you counted those three pairs of shoes.

Still, the headline was correct.

'Man Dances Self to Death'.

That, after all, is just what he did.

✤ Our Man in Geneva Wins a Million Euros ✤

Our man in Geneva sits before his computer and blinks at the messages in his inbox. 'Brother, size matters,' says a message from K. P. Rimmer. 'Give her an opportunity to spread rumours about your enormous size. Make her happy by delaying your explosions tonight.'

'Don't be a two-pump chump,' says Karl Lumsky. 'Millions of men are facing this issue, and the smartest ones already got an answer. Safe, efficient and covering all aspects, Extra-Time will help you forget the premature nightmare.'

'Do you realise superfluous body kilos kill more and more people around the world?' asks Joni Corona. 'We believe that you hate the unattractive look of those people and the social bias against them. Moreover, you've not the will to resist an assault of ruinous eating habits of yours. If it sounds familiar, then we have something for you!'

Our man is the Consular Officer at the Permanent Mission of the Republic of Zimbabwe to the United Nations Office in Geneva, which also serves as the country's embassy to Switzerland. At fifty-five and in his first foreign posting, he is a latecomer to the Internet and all its glories.

'Baba, get email,' his children said back in Harare. There was no need, he always said. Too expensive, too set in his ways.

In Geneva, the connection comes with his telephone line. Night after night finds him enmeshed in the World Wide Web, scrolling through emails spun in places he has never been, emails that are woven into his life and leave him blinking before his computer screen. He types slowly, with two fingers, his tongue between his teeth. 'Like a policeman typing a report on a burglary', his wife teases him, 'at the Charge Office in Harare.'

'See how easy communicating becomes,' says his daughter Susan in England. 'Don't forget to send the instalment for the next term.' She follows the sentence with several bouncing, bald, yellow, bodiless cartoon heads that open their mouths in toothless smiles as they wink at him.

'Baba, I need money,' is the echo from his son Robert in Canada.

'Improve your credit rating,' says Frederick Turk.

He is about to click on this message when he sees the next one.

'Important communication,' this message says, 'you are a winner!!' The message is from the European Bank of Luxembourg (EBL), headquarters – Brussels, Belgium. There is an attached letter on the bank's letterhead, signed by Dr E. S. Rose, Department Head (Corporate Affairs). In a circle around the name are twelve gold stars, just like the stars on the flag of the European Union.

'Greetings,' Dr Rose says, 'and congratulations. Your email has been entered into the EBL's annual lottery. You have been selected as one of ten winners to win €1,000,000 each. Write back quickly or lose this chance.'

Blood sings from his thumping heart to the rest of his body.

'Are you sure that it is me?' he types. 'I did not enter any lottery. Have I really won a million euros?'

'Your email was automatically entered by your Internet service provider,' says Dr Rose. 'You really have won a million euros.'

That is the explanation, he thinks, for Rimmer, Lumsky, Corona. And Turk, and Morgan, Shelby, Gordon. They got his email from his Internet service provider.

'How do I get the money?' he asks.

135

'You will hear from Mr George, our Chief of Client Accounts.'

Within an hour, Mr George writes and says, 'Greetings and congratulations. The million is yours to pick up at our offices in Amsterdam. We will charge you an administration fee of €5,000.'

Five thousand euros is a lot of money to pay in admin fees, he thinks, but it is a piffle compared to a million. In his head he does his sums: one euro is roughly two Swiss francs. He has six thousand francs just sitting in his bank account. It is for Susan's second term, but it is not due for another month. He can get four thousand on his credit card to make ten thousand. Almost exactly five thousand euros. This he sees as a sign of a larger truth: God's hand is in this matter, at the very heart of this good fortune.

For the first time in his life, he uses the Internet to book a flight. The secretary at the embassy recommends easyJet. He does not tell her about his bounty, he has not even told his wife. He wants to surprise her and the children with cold cash evidence of the magnificence of the Lord. His nightly prayers are more fervent than usual. For the Lord has looked upon His servant and found him worthy.

∾

The trip to Amsterdam is his first ever trip out of

Geneva. His only travels are when he goes from home in Petit Saconnex to the embassy in Chambesy, or drives up the gentle incline of the United Nations complex to attend meetings. On Saturdays, he drives his wife across the French border to shop at the Champion hypermarket. On Sundays, they drive to church. Thus he is not so well flown that he is entirely immune to the thrill of taking off from the ground to be enveloped in the clouds.

The last time that he was on an aeroplane was on his way to Geneva from Harare where his brothers saw him off at the airport. He has three brothers, one of whom lives in his old house in Waterfalls in Harare. When he calls his brother to check up on him, his family and the house, his sister-in-law hijacks the conversation with a repetitive litany of woe. Her talk is of power cuts, water cuts and rising bread prices. 'Not like you in Geneva,' she says. '*Vagoni muri ku*Switzer.'

He tries to inject his own miseries into the conversation. 'Can you believe we live in a flat, an apartment, they call it here,' he says, too loudly, too vehemently. 'Just a flat, *heh*? A flat, just like single people.' Feeling guilty for such a petty complaint. Knowing that, at least, he has three square meals a day. And electricity that allows him access to the Internet.

It is the grace of God that allowed him to escape the power cuts, the water cuts, the rising bread prices.

He is not a career diplomat. God picked him out of the passport office at Makombe Building in Harare, thrusting him out of the way of approaching penury, just in time to enable his children to go to universities in Canada and England. He reads the newspapers that are flown in every month from Harare. He is the least important member of staff at the embassy, after the secretaries and driver, so he gets them last. The secretaries and driver are local recruits; they do not care about the news from a place they will never call home. The fall in the Zimdollar does not see a corresponding rise in their blood pressure. So the newspapers end up piled up in his office.

Every editorial wages war against inflation. Government ministers treat it like it is something outside of themselves and their policies; they wage war on it, they proclaim it the public enemy number one, they launch offensives on different fronts. Every week, unnamed economists issue sunny predictions on the turnaround of the economy.

Inflation will go down.

From twenty-five million and five hundred thousand per cent.

Any time now.

Any time soon.

The President glowers from every front page.

∾

Like sex shops and pregnant women baring their stomachs in public in the summer, the Internet is a Geneva discovery. He knew of it, of course, but it did not feature much among *his* generation of civil servants. At the passport office in Harare where he was Head of the Department, everything was handwritten. And even here in Geneva, he does not use the computer at work. All typing is done by the secretary. He does not need the Internet for his work.

Then again, there is very little work.

Geneva is not London, or Johannesburg or Gaborone or Dallas, Texas, where there are hordes of Zimbabweans losing themselves or their passports, dying and getting arrested. There is not enough consular work to do, and even if there were, he is only a mailbox, an intermediary.

'I will send your papers to Harare,' he says to a woman who wants a passport for a newly born Zimbabwean. 'It will take up to eight months, in fact, it is faster if you go to Harare and apply from there.'

'So what are you here for?' she asks.

'It is faster in Harare,' he repeats.

She leaves without saying goodbye.

'In Zimbabwe, out of Zimbabwe, civil servants are all the same,' she says.

∾

139

He has learned the hard way that a first-world lifestyle demands a first-world salary. His monthly salary of six thousand two hundred francs a month would be adequate if only it were paid on time. After paying the rent, which is exactly a third of his salary, and paying the bills, and sending money back home, and by living on a diet of Champion value food, he and his wife save enough to put the children through university. Robert is finishing the third year, and Susan only just started.

He has recently been promoted from Full-Time Consular Officer to Part Consular Officer and Delegate. On seeing him wade through the piled-up newspapers, his Ambassador said to him, 'Attend meetings at WIPO. And take in ITU and OMM if Chinyanga is busy.'

He now spends his days at meeting after meeting at which people talk of compulsory licensing and layout designs and topographies of integrated circuits. They talk of possible amendments to Article 6*quinquies* of the Paris Convention. They talk of the Berne Convention and the Lisbon Convention and trade-related aspects of intellectual property rights. They laugh at jokes that he has no hope of ever understanding.

Other African delegates peel away the veneer of diplomacy on learning his nationality. They address

him with an affectionate familiarity. 'You Zimbabweans,' says the Kenyan delegate. 'You want to drive
out *muzungu, heh*?' The Kenyan delegate laughs, and
the Zambian and Tanzanian delegates join in.

'You Zimbabweans,' echoes the Ethiopian delegate. 'When are you getting rid of your President?
And our Mengistu, there in Harare with him?'

He develops a laugh for encounters such as these.

He learns to fall asleep with his eyes open.

∾

On the flight to Amsterdam, he dreams of a new
geyser for their house in Harare. The last time he
called home, his brother's wife said the old geyser is
giving problems. He must remember to ask his brother to call Tregers' for a quotation, he thinks. Then he
remembers that with a million euros, they can buy a
new house, *houses*, for him and his brothers. And
each of their children. And their children's children.

He works out how much a million euros is in
Zimbabwe dollars. Each euro is two million dollars,
on the parallel market, of course. 2,000,000,000,000
Zimbabwe dollars. His mind cannot expand enough
to take this in.

Twelve zeroes make a billion, according to the
United Kingdom system of counting. Twelve zeroes
make a trillion, going by the United States version.

141

Two billion or two trillion. One-fifth of Zimbabwe's last annual budget. A lot of money, in any country. In a flood of thanksgiving, he plans all the things he will buy for his Lord's representative on earth, their pastor in Harare.

A new cellphone, for sure.

A stove and a fridge.

A suit for the pastor.

An outfit (with a hat) for the pastor's wife.

Toys and clothes for their children.

In his mind he sees the pastor's children on his farewell visit, peering at the black-and-white cartoon images hissing from their fourth-hand television.

'I will buy them a new television,' he vows. 'One with a flat screen.'

❧

The grimy façade of the building that houses the European Bank of Luxembourg gives him pause. When he sees the broken elevator, the ten-franc ham sandwich that he ate on the flight moves uneasily in his stomach. He walks up the stairs to the second floor. A door with the letters EBL in black flourishes on a gold plaque gives him some reassurance. The door looks serious, solid. Inside, he finds that the offices are not as grimy as the outside indicated. The ham sandwich settles in his innards.

The biggest surprise is Mr George. He is not the white gentleman of our man's imagination, smiling with largess in a bustling office. Instead, he is a lone young man with a West African accent. He has several gold chains around his neck. He wears black denim jeans with giant pockets at the knees, patent leather shoes, and has two cellphones on his belt. He interrupts their conversation to talk in low tones on his phones. To our man who does not understand the language, the one-sided conversations sound vaguely sinister.

'The money you have won needs to be cleaned,' Mr George explains to him. 'And you need to give us twenty-five thousand euros for that purpose.' The word sounds like *papas*. 'We cannot give it to you in this state.' *In dis stet.* 'There is an expensive chemical that we must buy.' *Iks-pansive kamikal.*

Mr George takes a fifty-euro note. It has some markings on it, reddish brown, above the stars of Europe. He wipes it down with a cloth on which he has sprinkled a transparent fluid. The note emerges pristine. The term money-laundering comes from that part of our man's mind that absorbs the news and documentaries that he watches every night on BBC World. He asks the question.

'No, no, no.' Mr George laughs a full-bodied laugh that sees him click-clicking his fingers and clink-

clinking his gold chains. 'Money-laundering. No, no, no. That is for dirty money, money from prostitutes and drugs, money that is sent to accounts in Cayman Islands, you understand me? This is a lottery, you understand me? This no dirty money. God has chosen us to find people like you, to help you.'

Mr George pauses to answer the phone ringing on his right.

'Dr Rose, he wants to help you,' Mr George continues. 'He even mention your name especially, you understand me.'

Our man understands nothing, but the earlier reference to God settles in his mind. 'I am a civil servant,' he explains. 'I do not have twenty-five thousand euros. Can't you just deduct your money from my million euros before you give it to me?'

Mr George laughs.

Click-clickety, clink-clinkety.

'No, no, no. That is not how we do it, you understand me. But it's okay. If you don't trust me, we can't do business. You can take your five thousand, and lose your million euros.' Our man has already handed over the five thousand euros; they rest snugly in the back pocket of Mr George's jeans.

He can see their outline when Mr George turns.

'Here is what I propose. You are a nice guy, flown all this way. You can't leave empty-handed. We can lend it to you. Or rather, we have a partner who can lend it to you.' And he mentions a Miss Manning from Equity, Loan and Finance Company of London. *Lorn-dorn.*

Our man is dismayed to learn that he has to deal with yet another person in yet another city. 'You do not have to go to London,' Mr George says. 'Miss Manning will contact you to arrange the loan.'

Our man is bewildered by all of this. 'Why can't the bank just get the money directly from this lender? Why does the money need to be washed?' To all the whys, asked and unasked, Mr George has one response. 'Go back to Geneva, and await Miss Manning's email.'

∾

In Geneva, our man is anxious but not afraid. A week passes, and nothing happens. He emails Dr Rose who tells him to contact Mr George who tells him to await Miss Manning. Miss Manning finally contacts him, by email and then by post. The letter that comes by post says, 'Greetings. May our Lord Jesus Christ shower his Blessings upon you and all your Beloved. I looked into my heart and found a Blessed Peace. I pass this Peace on to you today. Herein please find a cheque for 25,000 euros, to be repaid on receiving your winnings.'

Our man is tempted to kiss the cheque, but restrains himself.

'Worship God, not Mammon.'

Within an hour, Mr George writes to him.

'Greetings,' he says. 'Please send us the money, as soon as the cheque clears. Your million will soon be in your account. Trust God.'

In two days, the cheque clears.

'Learn humility,' our man chides himself. He promises the Lord not to doubt His wisdom again. He sends the money to Mr George. He waits a day, two days, a week, two weeks. There is no news from Amsterdam, or Brussels. There is no news from London. *Lorn-Dorn.*

He emails Dr Rose, Mr George, Miss Manning, in that order, every day, twice a day for one week. Dr Rose finally responds in a letter of fluid persuasion. 'We would not cheat you, my friend,' the email says. 'As for me, I am a woman fearful of God. My promise is my credit.'

The reference to the possibility of cheating him does not alarm our man so much as Dr Rose's revelation that she is a woman. He finds himself back in Amsterdam, Mr George's voice in his ear. '*Dr Rose, he wants to help you. He even mention your name especially, you understand me.*'

'You say you are a woman,' our man writes. 'I thought you were a man. Mr George distinctly told me that you were a man. In Amsterdam, he said you were a man.'

'Make no assumptions, my friend,' Dr Rose responds. 'Only have faith and all will be well. You will hear from Mr George.'

Mr George is brief, to the point.

'We need more money for chemicals,' he writes. 'Miss Manning is sending you another cheque.'

Our man in Geneva protests, but his emails bounce into empty space.

ᥜ

Every night, and first thing in the morning, he sits before the computer. He jumps at the pinging sound that announces new email. He is bothered by a permanent dryness in his throat. Susan calls to remind his wife about her second semester fees.

'*Wototaura nababa vako*,' his wife says. 'He will send the money next week, that is, unless he has spent it all.' Our man joins in her laughter, his own laugh sounding to his ears like Mr George's.

'Spent the money? No, no, no.'

Click-clickety, clink-clinkety.

He opens his Bible to a random page. Like an answer to a prayer, his eyes fall on Jeremiah 33:3. 'Call unto me, and I will answer thee, and show thee great and mighty things, which thou knowest not.'

He asks God to show him the way. The Lord speaks to him with all the clarity of common sense. 'Forget about the million euros. Come clean to your wife. Pray together and work together. Write a letter to your daughter's university. Ask for a grace period. If necessary, take a loan from those credit people who send emails.' For the first time in weeks, our man sleeps the sleep of dreamless ease.

He wakes the next day with a sense of purpose. The morning is bright with hope. The clocks have moved up an hour, and the year is approaching spring. As he drives up the hill towards the United Nations, the sun casts its rays through the slits in the giant sculpture of the Broken Chair and into the windows of his car. The snow drips from the trees. The birds sing from the melting boughs. At the yellow and black zebra crossing just after the Broken Chair, he stops to allow a woman and her toddler to cross the street. The child drops its teddy bear, breaks free of its mother, runs back to pick it up and meets the eyes of our man through the windscreen. The child breaks into a toothless grin and waves. Our man waves back. He is seized by a burst of joy so intense that he almost gasps. As he drives on to Chambesy, he whistles his wife's favourite hymn of thanksgiving.

'*Simudza maoko ako, urumbidze Mwari, nekuti Ndiye ega akarurama.*'

148

His heart is filled with grace and gratitude.

In the afternoon, his bank manager asks to see him.

❧

'We need to discuss an irregular transaction from your account,' the bank manager says. 'You deposited a fraudulent instrument into your account. We cleared it, but the American bank on which the cheque was drawn has now refused to honour it.

'We would normally take the blame,' the bank manager says, 'but this does not apply to cheques drawn on American banks.'

Our man's stomach turns to water. 'Dr Rose and Mr George and Miss Manning,' he says. 'Dr Rose.'

The bank manager offers him a drink. He empties the glass in three swallows. Water dribbles from the glass onto his tie. He explains about the email that started it all, the trip to Amsterdam, the dirty money, the loan, the cheque. It takes eleven minutes. He contradicts himself three times.

He drinks a litre of water.

'This is clearly a matter for the police,' the manager says. 'It is difficult to establish identity in such cases. For all we know, this could be the work of just one person. It often is.'

The full meaning of the manager's words hits our man. 'I can take you to Amsterdam,' he says. 'We can go there together. I'll pay for our tickets. We can catch Mr George. Write to Dr Rose. I have their emails. Write to Dr Rose.'

'That is not the bank's immediate concern,' the bank manager says. 'I called you to give you this.' Our man takes the proffered paper. It is a letter of demand. The amount of fifty-one thousand two hundred and thirty-four Swiss francs, equivalent to twenty-five thousand euros, is to be repaid within thirty days. He looks at the bank manager's face, looking to find something that says the letter is not real. He does not find what he seeks. He swallows.

From a very far-off place comes a voice that sounds like the bank manager's. The voice sounds like it has travelled a long way and echoes around the room. 'I will call the police for you,' the voice says.

Police, police, the word is loud in our man's head. His mother's voice speaks across time and space: 'You take any more of that sugar, and I will call the police.' That memory sparks another, and suddenly, there they all are; his mother and his uncle Benkias, his sister Shupikai holding his son at age two, all of them crowding his head. 'I will call them now,' the bank manager says. As the bank manager reaches for the telephone, our man reaches for water, but the glass is empty, the bottle too.

∾ The Maid from Lalapanzi ∾

'You should not play outside in the rain when you are wearing red,' *Sisi*Blandina said to Munya and me.

'Lightning likes things that are red and it will hunt you out and strike you down and burn you from inside out.

'And you must not sit out on the road, otherwise you will grow festering boils on your bottoms.

'You should never cut your hair out of doors, because if even the smallest fluff is left in the open, *varoyi* will find it, and put a spell on you, and you know how powerful their sorcery is.

'And you must not peek at each other while you dress, because boys and girls who spy on each other's nakedness get styes in their eyes.'

She told story upon story of the fates that awaited us if we did things we were not supposed to do, and she had the proof, for these things had happened to people she knew in Lalapanzi.

'You must not walk over a person's legs,' *Sisi*Blandina said. 'If you do so, you must walk back the other way to reverse the action, and if you don't, the one who has been walked over won't grow.'

I made Munya lie on his back. I jumped over his legs and out of the house to play. He ran to find *Sisi*Blandina and wailed, 'Chenai jumped me. She always jumps me, and now I won't grow.'

*Sisi*Blandina marched out of the house, with Munya sniffling beside her. Her nails dug into my flesh as she grabbed me above my right elbow and dragged me from my play.

'You will not go outside until you walk back over him,' she said.

I obeyed, jumping over him, but making sure that I crossed my fingers on both hands behind my back.

'She had nings on,' my brother cried. 'It won't work because Chenai crossed her fingers, she had nings on.'

'Nings nings, *chii chacho*,' *Sisi*Blandina said. 'Why must you always believe what those white children tell you? Did their parents not lose the war?'

That was incontrovertible, it was unanswerable.

We *had* won the war, we had conquered the conquerors. Our parents said it all the time. The television said it, the radio too. We had won the war.

Munya, who had been torn between the binding

nature of nings and the authority of *Sisi*Blandina, now believed her when she said that he would grow as tall as my father.

'Bigger,' he said. 'I want to be bigger than *Sekuru*Thomas.'

'You will be bigger and stronger too,' she said.

'Will I be like Mr T, from *The A-Team*?'

'Exactly like Mr T,' she said.

She petted him, and said she would take him to the shops to buy sweets with her own money. Now that the threat of dwarfism had been thwarted, Munya could afford to be generous. 'I will bring you Treetop sherbet,' he said.

I could still see the marks that *Sisi*Blandina had dug into my arm.

'Keep your stupid sherbet,' I fumed as I stormed off to pour water all over the shiny kitchen floor. When *Sisi*Blandina smacked me across my bottom I screamed, 'You are not my mother; you are only the housemaid.'

'Yes,' she said. 'I am only the housemaid, but your mother is not here.'

❦

My mother was often not there because she had day shifts and night shifts as a nurse at Andrew Fleming, later called Parirenyatwa Hospital. I was not always happy when she *was* home because she pulled my hair when she plaited it, which made me wince in pain and sit with my face tight for two days before the plaits settled on my head. She spanked me hard when I made Munya cut my hair so that she could not plait and yank it any more.

My father was there and not there, and when he was, he sometimes looked at Munya and me like he wasn't sure what we were doing in front of him. He smoked Kingsgate cigarettes and we liked to watch him blow smoke rings in the air. He taught mathematics at the university, and when Munya asked why we could not have a dog because everyone had a dog, Daddy drew him something that he said was a model that proved that it was rationally and statistically impossible for everyone in the world to have a dog.

So mostly, we had *Sisi*Blandina to look after us. She had my mother's authority to command, and reward, to cajole, threaten and smack us in accordance with her judgement. She came from Lalapanzi, *Sisi*Blandina, smack in the middle of the country, a place so central that the province in which it rested was called the Midlands. In Lalapanzi, the lightning hunted out little girls and boys who played in the rain in red, it sought their red clothes and burned them from inside out. The rivers of Lalapanzi were home to *njuzu*, fearsome water creatures that sometimes took children and made them live under water. In Lalapanzi wandered a *goritoto*, a ghost giant that cast a shadow of bright light as it moved.

∾

The government renamed the places that the whites had renamed, so that Umvukwes became Mvurwi again, Selukwe became Shurugwi, and Marandellas became Marondera. Queque became Kwekwe. The changes did not affect people like my grandmother for whom independence was a reality that did not alter their memories. She continued to speak of Fort Victoria and not Masvingo, of visiting us in Salisbury when she meant Harare, and of my aunt who was married in Gwelo instead of Gweru. *Sisi*Blandina was not as bad as my grandmother, but like most people then, she sometimes forgot to use the new names.

'To get to Lalapanzi,' *Sisi*Blandina said, 'you take the train here in Salisbury and get off at Gwelo. You then take a bus from Gwelo and drive through Wha Wha before you get to Lalapanzi.'

I liked to work the rhythm of the names into my skipping games.

> '*Right foot Salisbury, left foot Gwelo.*
> *Right foot Gwelo, left foot Wha Wha.*
> *Right foot Wha Wha, left foot Lalapanzi.*

157

Right foot Lalapanzi, left foot Lalapanzi.
Both feet Lalapanzi, both feet Lalapanzi.'

∾

There had been many housemaids before *Sisi*-Blandina. They lived with us, they were a part of our family and yet were not of it, sharing my bedroom, and getting up at five in the morning to sweep the floors, make the breakfast for my parents and for Munya and me, wash the dishes, walk Munya and me to school, wash the clothes and the windows, make lunch for Munya and me, fetch us from school, do the lunchtime dishes, make and serve the supper, wash more dishes, and through it all, watch that Munya and I behaved and didn't kill each other, before collapsing to wake again at five the next morning.

The white children like my old best friend Jenny Russell and Laura Steele in Miss Blakistone's class called the maids who worked at their houses by their first names, but we called them *Sisi*, sister, it being unthinkable that young children could address adults just by their first names. They came and went, dismissed for various flaws as my mother searched for the perfect housemaid, leaving behind the uniform dress and matching hat that they all wore which seemed to stretch and shrink to fit each one.

My mother dismissed *Sisi*Memory and *Sisi*Sekesai

158

because they ate too much bread in the morning, spooning too much jam on their bread.

'Housemaids should not eat too much,' said my mother.

*Sisi*Loveness dimpled and glowed when she smiled, and every Saturday she undid her plaited hair, scratched out the dandruff with a red plastic comb, washed her hair and plaited it again in neat rows across her head. She used Ingram's Camphor Cream and not normal Vaseline, and her clean smell lingered in every room that she left. My mother fired her because she said *Sisi*Loveness cared too much for her appearance and not enough for the floors of the house. I see now that my mother fired *Sisi*Loveness because she was all too aware of the stories of maids who stole husbands away from their employers.

'Housemaids should not be too pretty,' all the women agreed.

*Sisi*Dudzai was fired because my mother came home unexpectedly and found her dancing to *Bhutsu mutandarikwa*, sweating and dancing, as my mother said, like one possessed, stomping on the living room floor, clapping herself on in encouragement, head thrown back in abandonment, whistling like she was out herding cows.

'Housemaids should not enjoy themselves too much,' my mother declared.

Those who were not fired quit, like *Sisi*Maggie who left to get married to *Mukoma*Joseph, the gardener who worked for Mr Shelby from number twenty-five. The union did not bring Mr Shelby closer to us, and he still watched with an unfriendly face as Munya and I walked past his house, and grunted his response when we chirped, 'Good morning, Mr Shelby,' while Munya looked at Mr Shelby's dog Buster with longing.

*Sisi*Nomathemba quit because she could not make us obey her. Munya and I had an unerring eye for the weaknesses in the maids' resolve. We found them in *Sisi*Nomathemba, and sometimes led her away from the normal route along the road, and got her lost among the greenways at the back of the houses and left her there. We tormented and laughed at her because she spoke Ndebele, we said '*hai*' to everything she said because that was how she began her sentences, and we repeated what she said and mimicked her accent until, conquered, she wept and said *abantwana laba bayahlupha sibili*.

We went with *Sisi*Jenny to our mother's friend's niece's wedding in Canaan between Jerusalem and Engineering in Highfields and she wore a yellow dress with white stars that was too small for my mother. When the master of ceremonies pointed to the lorry that would drive people to the rural home of the bride, *Sisi*Jenny hurtled off in that direction and the last we saw of her was a distant figure in a yellow dress clambering into the packed lorry, her red shoe almost falling from her right foot.

*Sisi*Jenny was succeeded by *Sisi*Lucia, who was not pretty, and did not eat too much, and did not enjoy herself at all. She did not smile once in the two months that she was with us; she watched me all the time, and made me feel guilty for no reason. My mother thought she had found the perfect house-maid until *Sisi*Lucia locked Munya and me up in my bedroom and vanished with my mother's new electric kettle and toaster from Barbour's, her favourite pair of shoes and three pairs of my father's trousers.

My mother then tried out poor relations as maids. They came from the rural areas with the musty smell of old smoke on their clothes and the sweet smell of peanut oil on their skin. They delighted in the television and stood mesmerised before its images. *Vatete*Susan sat and watched as the Capwells in *Santa Barbara* failed to see that Dominic who whispered his words and appeared only in the shadows was really their supposedly dead mother Sophia, as evil Angela Channing tightened her grip on the Gioberti wine estate on *Falcon Crest*, and all the while my mother muttered under her breath and the fat congealed on the dishes piled up in the kitchen sink.

The Capwells did find out about Dominic/Sophia and Angela Channing lost to Chase Gioberti, but *Vatete*Susan was not there: she had been replaced by *Mbuya*Stella who liked to stretch out her legs on the floor as she talked through the smoke rings and regaled my bemused father with the latest stories of the antics of the black sheep of their family. Through the convoluted logic of Karanga relationships, at seventeen, she was his mother, and therefore my mother's mother-in-law, to be treated with some respect.

Then my mother decided that it was youth and not the lack of a blood connection that was the problem; the girls were too young, too inexperienced. She found instead a woman much older than her whom we called Auntie in the English way because she was not our relative but was too old to be called by her first name even if it was prefaced by *Sisi*, and whom my grandmother being hard of hearing called Kauntie. Kauntie fell asleep in the middle of the day and forgot to fetch Munya from school and he went hunting for tadpoles in the Chisipite stream, fell and banged his mouth and that was the end of his upper incisor tooth and of Kauntie. And that is how we ended up with *Sisi*Blandina, who spoke Karanga as deep as my grandmother's, and after two years it was almost like she had always been there.

❧

When *Sisi*Blandina told us stories that her grandmother had told her, she began the tales in the traditional manner and said *ngano ngano ngano*, lilting the
different syllables, and we replied *ngano*, and she
repeated it twice to make sure we were really ready; we
chanted back to her in anticipation because we knew
that she would lead us to an enchanted realm where
boys who turned into lions won the maidens of their
hearts' desire, the hare was more cunning than his
uncle the baboon, the girl who scorned to squeeze an
ugly old woman's sores ended up living in enchant-
ment beneath the water, and the king of a land far
away set a trap to find which of his perfidious wives
and children had cooked and eaten his royal tortoise.

My mother liked *Sisi*Blandina for different reasons. She did things without being told like arrang-
ing the clothes in all our cupboards according to
colour and polishing the floors with Cobra polish
with such vigour that my father complained that
they were too slippery and my mother said he should
buy the fitted carpets that she had set her heart on.
Instead, my father said, 'Well, well, we may as well
invite the Prime Minister to hold his next rally here
and not to bother with Rufaro or Gwanzura,' because
*Sisi*Blandina sang songs from the war as she bathed
and scrubbed her skin with a pumice stone.

❧

Munya and I knew that there had been a war, but it was only through *Sisi*Blandina that it came to life in our house. She told us stories of the war, the guerrillas marching to her village in Lalapanzi and demanding food, the soldiers following the guerrillas and threatening to shoot the villagers who gave the guerrillas food, and then more guerrillas coming and threatening to shoot all *vatengesi*, traitors who sold them out to the soldiers or refused to give them food. They shot into the air to frighten people, and when her grandmother's dog Pfungwadzebenzi barked, a guerrilla shot him in the stomach and he limped off to the forest to die. Munya put his hand on *Sisi*Blandina's knee and said, 'When Chenai grows up and buys me a dog, I won't call him Spider, but Pfungwadzebenzi.'

She told us that the villagers stayed up all night in a *pungwe*, a night rally at which guerrilla commanders with bushy beards denounced the Smith regime, told them about *gutsaruzhinji*, the socialism they would bring upon ending the days of Smith. Their voices were hoarse as the villagers chanted the new slogans and sang the new revolutionary songs, while young men with rifles danced to those same songs that *Sisi*Blandina taught us.

> '*What to do with Smith?*
> *Hit him on the head until he comes to his senses!*
> *What to do with the ugly crow?*

Hit him on his head until he comes to his senses!
What to do with Muzorewa?
Hit him on the head until he comes to his senses!
Until when?
Until we rule this country of Zimbabwe!'

I remembered that for the first five years of my life, I lived in a country called Rhodesia with Ian Smith as Prime Minister, and then in Zimbabwe-Rhodesia with a Prime Minister called Abel Muzorewa, and now the country was called Zimbabwe and Robert Mugabe was Prime Minister. As for Munya, born on the cusp of independence, just one year away from being among the special born-frees, the songs meant nothing at all.

And so we held our own *pungwes* in my bedroom with Munya and me taking on the role of the villagers and *Sisi*Blandina as our commander; we played out the stories that we thought had happened only in Lalapanzi.

❧

'I learned even more songs at the camp in Mozambique,' *Sisi*Blandina said. 'The guerrillas came back and asked for young boys and girls to go with them to be trained and we went all the way through to Chimoio and Nyadzonia in Mozambique.'

We sang those training camp songs as *Sisi*Blandina walked Munya and me to school, swinging our arms

165

in hers while we swung our book cases on the other
arms; we marched to their rhythm and chanted *hau*
as she led us in our favourite song, the one we asked
for over and over again.

> '*We shall go from here (hau)*
> *And head for Moza (hau)*
> *Yugoslavia (hau)*
> *And China (hau)*
> *They shall give us (hau)*
> *An arsenal of weapons (hau)*
> *To take with us (hau)*
> *To Lancaster House (hau)*
> *Do you doubt us? (hau)*
> *Do you doubt us? (hau)*'

'Everyone took a new name, a war name, a strong
name,' *Sisi*Blandina said. 'I wanted to call myself
Freedom, but there were already seven with that
name, and even one called Freedom-now, and four
other people called Liberty. Then one of the commanders told us that we were fighting for autonomy
and for self-rule and for self-determination, and so
that became my name.'

'That is a long name,' I said in wonder.

*Sisi*Blandina laughed and said, 'No, just Autonomy.
I am Blandina Autonomy Mubaiwa. Some of us girls
were trained to fight, but the younger ones like me,

and some who could not do the exercises, cooked for the guerrillas and washed their clothes and we sang and we kept them company at night. But the first night, they said I was in Geneva, and they sent me back to the other girls who were also in Geneva.'

'Is Geneva in Mozambique?' my brother asked.

'That is not for you to know,' she said. 'Your sister will know soon enough. See, already her breasts are poking out.'

I stormed off without hearing more, furious that she had voiced my deepest shame. My breasts had started to sprout three months earlier, and I walked with a stoop to hide them. I thought no one had noticed, but *Sisi*Blandina noticed everything. When my period came, *Sisi*Blandina was there to say, 'Well, you are in Geneva now, and you will be visiting regularly. Better make sure those boys you like to play with keep themselves to themselves.'

I was mortified because I knew what she was talking about. The women from Johnson & Johnson had come to the school, and separated us from the boys so that they could tell us secrets about our bodies. They said the ovum would be released from the ovary and travel down the Fallopian tube and, if it was not fertilised, it would be expelled every twenty-two to twenty-eight days in the act of menstruation. It was an unsanitary time, they said. Our most effective weapon against this effluence was the arsenal of the sanitary products that Johnson & Johnson made with young ladies like us in mind, they said, because Johnson cared.

⚘

I came to know many things about *Sisi*Blandina. I spied on her and read her letters; I read the ones she wrote before she posted them, letters written in her small rounded handwriting, letters with long elaborate beginnings and little news. 'Chenai is growing breasts,' she said in one, and I was angry that she would tell my secrets to people in Lalapanzi. I tore up the letter, and dropped it to the floor. Sometimes, she cried, for no reason at all, and I heard her when I woke up late at night in our bedroom.

⚘

She had admirers at the shops and all the gardeners in our road whistled if they were out in the road when she walked past. Even *Mukoma*Joseph who worked for Mr Shelby from number twenty-five and had married *Sisi*Maggie and sent her off to the rural areas said in his lisp, '*Ende* sister *makabatana*, you are so well put together.'

She ignored *Mukoma*Joseph and the others and talked only to *Mukoma*George who worked at the

Post Office and who made sure to watch for us as we walked past.

'Ah, hello sister Chenai, hello *mfana*Munya, *masikati masikati*,' he said.

'*Masikati Mukoma*George,' we greeted him back.

'*Hesi kani*, Blandina,' he said.

'*Ho nhai*, so I am the one that you greet last?' she said.

'Last but not least, Blandina, you know that,' he said.

They lingered and talked while Munya and I moved ahead of them. One day, *Mukoma*George ran after me as I walked home alone from recorder practice.

He said, 'Ah, *masikati* sister Chenai, please take this to Blandina,' and thrust a blue aerogramme and a packet of Treetop sherbet into my hands.

The sherbet was for me, he said, and I ate it on the way home. *Sisi*Blandina laughed when she read the aerogramme and said, '*Haiwa*, I have no time for such foolishness.' She would not let me read it, but I knew that she would keep it in a shoebox that she kept at the bottom of our cupboard with the other letters that she received from Lalapanzi, and that night I sneaked into her box and read it.

'My sweetheart Blandina,' *Mukoma*George had written,

Time, fortune and opportunity have forced me to take up my hand to pen this missive to ask how are you pulling the wagons of existence and to tell you how much I love you. My heart longs for you like tea longs for sugar. I wish for you like meat wishes for salt, and I miss you like a postman would miss his bicycle. Truly, Blandina, you are my life, and I hope that you will be my wife. I want to send a messenger to Lalapanzi with any cows that your father asks as a bride price. I hope one day to be your ever-loving husband,

George Simbarashe Gweme from Munyikwa

After that letter, *Sisi*Blandina lingered more and more with *Mukoma*George as she walked us back home from school. She now took all her Sundays off, she went away early in the morning, and then one Sunday she did not come back and that was the only time my mother ever had to shout at her. She made herself three new dresses on her sewing machine.

She talked less and less about the war.

'Is Princess a nicer name than Rosemary?' she said. 'Do you like Precious or Prudence? What about George for a boy?'

When I said that she should ask *Mukoma*George if he liked it, she laughed and sang me another war song.

Then one day, just like that, she was gone.

She went for her Sunday off, and called my mother in the evening to say she would come for her clothes.

She was getting married she said, she was going to elope to *Mukoma*George's aunt's house in Engin-eering. She came back to pack up her things, her sewing machine, and box of letters, and her three pairs of shoes, her pleated skirt with the cloth belt, her two blouses and her two-piece costume that my mother had given her, and the three dresses that she had made on her sewing machine. The only thing she left behind was the uniform dress and matching hat on her bare shelf in the middle of my wardrobe.

Three weeks after she left us, there was a clanging sound from our gate, and the dogs from next door barked at the sound and there was *Sisi*Blandina. She cried as she told my mother that George asked why it had taken so long for her to go to him if she was sure the child was his and anyway, George said, he had a girl in Munyikwa who was promised to him. *Sisi*Blandina told my mother that she told him he had deceived her and then he said he could not marry someone who was not a maiden and she said but he knew all the time because she told him about the camp in Mozambique and how she kept the guerrillas company and my mother said Blandina, and *Sisi*Blandina said but it was not my fault that is what we were told to do and my mother said *ndine*

171

urombo Blandina, I feel pity, but you cannot stay here when things are like this, and *Sisi*Blandina wept and said, I have nowhere to go and my mother said you can go back to Lalapanzi and *Sisi*Blandina said oh God, my father, she said how will I face my father, and my mother said I can give you some money for the first few months but you cannot stay here and *Sisi*Blandina wept and stayed the night but left before I woke up the next morning and I never saw her again.

~

The police came to our house on the same day that my mother's sister, my aunt from Gwelo, came to visit and they said that a woman had been taken out of the Mukuvisi River and did my parents know her because she had an aerogramme in her bag with our address on it. My father went with them and identified *Sisi*Blandina and he came back and told my mother. She cried and my aunt said to her, well, this is what happens when you try to help these girls and she said something about whores who slept with men to whom they were not married. Then she said to my father, really, these maids are all the same.

∾ Aunt Juliana's Indian ∾

Mr Vaswani of Vaswani Brothers General Dealers was the first Indian that I saw closely enough to count the teeth in his mouth and the buttons on his shirt. I had seen Indians before; they were hard to miss, the women in fabrics of gossamer lightness, splashes of colour on Salisbury's pavements, and, like their men, as brown as we but with hair that slipped and slithered like white people's. Until I saw Mr Vaswani, I had never been close enough to them to see the colour of their irises.

Our school in Chitsa was closed because of the war so that my brother Danai and I were sent to Glen Norah Township in Salisbury to live with my mother's younger sister, *Mainin'*Juliana, who shared a house with their brother, our *Sekuru*Lazarus. We came to know all about *Mainin'*Juliana's Indian. She called him *Mu*India *wangu*, my Indian, shorthand for my Indian employer, to distinguish him from all the other Indians that were not Mr Vaswani. She worked in a shop in town that sold everything an African could possibly need, she said.

'I stand behind the counter and help the shoppers,' she told us. 'And all he does is to stand there ordering me about. It is always Juliana you are wary, wary slow, and Juliana hurry up, hurry up because there are wary, wary many customers.'

*Mainin'*Juliana argued with our neighbour's daughter Susan, who worked in a white family's house in the suburbs.

'*Mu*India *wangu* is a difficult man,' said *Mainin'*Juliana.

'My white madam is more difficult,' said Susan.

'He waits until the last possible moment before paying our salaries.'

'*Manje* madam *vangu* lies in bed all day and smokes while I clean.'

'He shouts at me, all day in my ear.'

'She won't let me eat any leftovers, imagine, her dog eats better than me. *Ufunge*, she even rides with her dog in front with her in the truck, and me in the back with all the sun and dust.'

'He won't advance me money to do my Pitman's examinations. Just fifteen dollars, imagine.'

'She won't allow her husband to put electricity in the boy's *kaya*, so I have to cook outside.'

'He talks all day and sometimes won't let me have my lunch.'

'Madam *vangu* is too lazy even to wash her own underwear; I have to do it by hand.'

'One of these days,' vowed *Mainin'*Juliana, 'I am going to punch those spectacles off his nose.'

❧

Danai and I decided that when we grew up, we would work for *Mu*India rather than the white madam. We spoke of him in one breath as *Mu*India *waMainin'*Juliana, and talked of him as intimately as we did the members of our very large family, wondering at the peculiar singularity of his ways, his refusal to advance salaries even when there was illness in the family, his habit of picking his nose when he thought that no one was looking, the leftover Zambia cloth and bent out of shape Kango plates and cups with missing handles that he gave Juliana and his other assistant, Timothy, as Christmas bonuses, the yellow plastic comb that he tucked behind his ear and next to his hair, and his house in Belvedere, which we pronounced Bharabhadhiya.

We became experts on Indians. *Mainin'*Juliana was not the only one with an Indian connection; our long-dead *Sekuru*Simplicious, who was the sibling between our mother and *Sekuru*Lazarus, had worked with Indians in Durban in South Africa before returning home to Rhodesia and dying in the war.

Indians did not wipe their bottoms with tissues: they washed them with water with their left hand. They worshipped cows. They did not eat meat. When they died, their bodies were burned and not buried. All their food contained curry. They all owned shops; and as shopkeepers, they were all just like *Mu*India who gave Juliana no Christmas bonus, but instead, gave her leftover pieces of Zambia cloths that no one wanted to buy. The pieces were rarely long enough to wrap around my eleven-year-old waist, and so Juliana gave them to our maternal grandmother who seemed to have a use for every piece of fabric she came across.

Out in Domboshava where my grandmother lived, the pieces of cloth increased my grandmother's consequence in the eyes of her neighbours. '*Akadii zvake Mu*India *wa*Juliana?' she would ask after his health. 'And has Juliana given him the herbs that I brought the last time that I was there?'

*Mu*India *waMainin'*Juliana's indigestion was of particular concern to her because it seemed never to end.

'Why does he not eat *sadza rerukweza*?' she asked, referring to a mud-brown traditional dish that required a strong stomach to eat.

178

'You and your *rukweza*,' said my uncle.

'It is not meat, so he can eat it.' And she launched into her usual lecture about the benefits of *sadza rerukweza* which opened up the intestines and allowed them to breathe.

'As my brother Simplicious who died in 1974 always said,' said *Sekuru*Lazarus, 'the problem with Indians is that they eat curry too much. Always they say *pili pili fakile*.'

At the same time that we admired our dead *Sekuru*Simplicious as a much-travelled man, Danai and I were surprised that the Indian language sounded so close to the little that we knew of Ndebele.

❧

*Mainin'*Juliana saw her job as no more than a bridging measure until she landed her dream job. 'I want to be a top-flight secretary,' she said to anyone who would listen.

She bought used books with broken spines that proclaimed themselves as having belonged to Tracy Thompson and Debbie Moffat and Squiffy Stevens. In the evenings, she hammered out on a typewriter with a missing m, pressing down on the keys, but with no paper because she could afford neither it nor the typewriter ribbon. She listened to records from the Rapid Results College. There was a single called

'Spoken English' that I played for Danai with the gramophone switch in the groove meant for LPs, so that the needle dragged across the record and the voices sounded deeply low and slow, even the woman's as she said, 'I want to speak good English.'

'She wants to speak good English,' said the man.

'I speak bad English.'

'She speaks bad English.'

'It is very hot in Spain.'

'She says that it is very hot in Spain.'

Her Rapid Results English proved unnecessary in her job; from what she told us, her real value was in translating *Mu*India's shouted orders to his customers to softer, more polite Shona.

*Mainin'*Juliana's top-flight dream seemed close to her in the middle of 1978, the year of the changes. We learned on the news that the government would build more schools and bring electricity to the townships. Danai and I made games out of the cartoon strips in the *Herald* newspaper and *Parade* magazine and played being Sam and Ben, characters created by the government to exhort people to vote.

'Sam,' Danai would say, 'if I vote in the April 1979 one man, one vote elections, what will I get?'

In a voice dripping with sincerity, I asked, 'What have you always wanted, Ben?'

'Majority Rule!'

'That is what you will get.'

'I also want peace; the war to stop.'

'That is what you will get.'

'I want the schools to open again; education for my children.'

'That is what you will get.'

'I want hospitals and clinics, good care for my family when they are sick.'

'That is what you will get.'

'There must be good jobs so we can earn good money.'

'When you vote that is what you will get.'

Then all together, we said, 'We must use our vote so that we can get our Majority Rule. We will both vote in the April 1979 one man, one vote elections.'

*Sekuru*Lazarus had much to say on these elections, as on every other subject. He spoke loudly and at length, *kupaumba* like my grandmother said, referring to the ceaseless sound that a drum makes in the hands of a particularly enthusiastic drummer, speaking always in a tone of argument even with those who agreed with him.

'Where were all the schools and the electricity all this time? You tell me that. The suburbs where the whites live are bright and clean, and we have, what? Now that the blacks have said no to their nonsense and taken up arms, do they think they can buy us with their electricity and their schools?

'We have said no, *aiwa, bodo, hwi, nikisi, kwete, haikona, tsvo.*

'They want to cloak our faces with deception. These are bribes to make us forget our suffering so that we vote for their internal settlement.

'I swear by my grandfather Musekiwa who died in 1959, I swear that even if all the townships in Rhodesia become white with light, I will never vote for Muzorewa.

'And if this finger on my left had not been cut off in 1965, I would have taken up arms, me.

'You would have seen me then.'

❧

The new schools that were being built then meant an end to hot-seating, which had meant that we remained at home while others used our classrooms, and then we went to school in the afternoon. Now, we were to go to a new school, one of the three in the township that had been built across the river. A new school meant new uniforms. *Mainin'*Juliana said we should come to town to buy our school uniforms from *Mu*India because she would get a discount.

Mr Vaswani's shop was at the corner of Bank Street and Manica Road, in the section of the city that was called *kuMa*India. As we passed by a dusty-looking shop with a dressmaker's dummy in the window and a dark interior, Juliana said, 'In there is the tailor who makes suits for the Prime Minister.'

I tried to imagine Prime Minister Smith with his sheep's eye walking *kuMa*India to have his suits made. He would have bumped into Africans, the women carrying bundles of shopping on their heads. He would have seen the Indians that we saw, and a few Coloureds, but he would have seen almost no Europeans, his would have been one of the few white faces. If he crossed the road, he would step into the road to Market Square and into a bus that took him to Mbare and from there to the rural areas. And if he continued walking down Manica Road and turned left at Inez Terrace, or walked up Baker Avenue or Gordon Avenue, he would end up in First Street facing the splendour of Barbour's Department Store and all the other shops like Miltons' and Thomas Meikle's where only white people like him did their shopping. Try as I could, I could not see the Prime Minister in this noise and chatter, and I thought, as *Sekuru*Lazarus sometimes said, 'Aunt Juliana tends to exaggerate matters.'

Mr Vaswani's shop was in a building that had carved pillars, and a veranda that read VASWANI BROTHERS GENERAL DEALERS EST. 1921. Above us were rows and rows of bicycles hanging from the ceiling, I had never seen so many Black Beauties assembled in one place. Blankets were stacked in piles while the bolts of Zambia material formed column upon column of riotous colour. There were piles of Kango plates, pots and pans, the metal cups that burned your mouth if you didn't wait for the tea to cool before you drank; there were grey metal buckets, metal dishes, and columns of heavy *bhodho* pots. And there, in plastic sheets with ENBEE printed on them, were school uniforms for all the schools in all the townships of Salisbury.

In the middle of all this was Mr Vaswani.

He looked straight at me, and I looked down, but not before I had glimpsed through the smoke that surrounded him the yellowing circles of his eyes, the brown teeth, the shiny buttons on his shirt, and the plastic comb yellow against his hair's slick blackness.

'How old are you?' he said.

I was tongue-tied, I had not expected him to speak to me so directly, but I managed to say, 'I am eleven and he is nine.'

'Wary good, wary good,' he said. 'You must work wary hard, okay. No room for layabouts in this world. Maybe you work for me, hey, and I employ Juliana's whole family.'

He did not speak English like we did, but nor did he sound like the white doctor who injected Danai and me at the Mission Hospital near Chitsa. He laughed to show more brown teeth right to the back of his mouth. I wondered whether he did not, after all, eat *sadza rerukweza*, like my grandmother said he should.

*Mainin'*Juliana pointed us to a bench in the corner and Danai and I studied him from there, hoping to see him pick his nose. His wife was with him at the counter. I watched in fascination as she walked behind the counter without once loosening the cloth around her body. I sniffed the air for curry, but all I could smell was Brylcreem and sweat and rubber and Lifebuoy and Perfection soap and the smell of the new things that were sold in the shop.

Like the Devure River near my aunt Vongai's homestead at Christmas when the rains were at their heaviest, Mr Vaswani's words were a constant flood. He aimed this flow at *Mainin'*Juliana as much as at the customers who took their time scrutinising every purchase before reluctantly handing over the money. 'Hurry up, hurry up,' he said. 'We haven't got all day.' His words were so like what *Mainin'*Juliana always said he said that I had to stop myself from giggling. Mr Vaswani noticed a woman who was struggling to take the clothes off her squirming son.

'Now, now, now, what is this, what is this?' he said. 'What is this?'

The woman ignored him and made the child strip off his clothes to try on a uniform. He wriggled in embarrassment, while his mother laughed as though she had not heard Mr Vaswani. 'He is mad, *Mu*India *uyu*,' she said to *Mainin'*Juliana and pointed at Mr Vaswani with her chin. 'How can I buy a uniform without my son trying it on?'

She yanked off her son's shirt; he held on to his shorts, and received a tongue-lashing from his mother. When the shorts came off, only his mother seemed unsurprised to find that he wore no underwear, and she talked on, while Danai and I pretended not to have seen the tears of shame that shone in the little boy's eyes.

Another woman came in with shorts and a shirt in two different sizes. 'No return, no refund,' said Mr Vaswani, pointing to a sign that said NO CREDIT NO RETURN NO REFUND in black letters on a white board. 'You buy the goods *foos-toos*.' She only stopped shouting when a white man entered the shop together with a black man dressed in gumboots and a blue boiler suit stiff with newness.

'Sanjiv,' the white man said, 'we want another bike.'

'Oh, Mr Johnson, you wary, wary good customer.' Mr Vaswani laughed with his mouth and his arms and his head. He tried to get the bicycle down himself but even on the ladder he could not quite reach it, and Timothy had to go up and help him.

'Sanjiv, why are Indians not allowed to play football?' the white man said.

Mr Vaswani revealed his teeth and said, 'Ah, another good joke, Mr Johnson. Always you tell funny jokes.'

Mr Johnson said, 'If they are given a corner, they build a shop. Get it, corner, shop, corner shop.'

'Wary funny, Mr Johnson,' said Mr Vaswani, 'Wary good joke indeed. Give a corner, build a shop.' He laughed again with his mouth and arms and head. Mrs Vaswani sent tinkles in accompaniment. The man in the boiler suit slapped his thigh as he laughed without a sound. Mr Johnson laughed some more as he left the shop. The man in the boiler suit followed with his Black Beauty, the knuckles of his hands prominent as he clutched the handles. As soon as they left, Mr Vaswani's smile left his face as if it had never been. 'Hurry up, hurry up,' he said. 'We haven't got all day.'

❦

Soon after our visit to the shop, elections were held in the townships for the first time. There were posters everywhere and placards with Bishop Muzorewa's four principles: nationalism for the people, democracy for the people, livelihood for the people, peace for the people, with his party's symbol of a hoe crossing a spear against the background of a shield.

*Sekuru*Lazarus's face became sourer with every poster that he saw.

'This is not true independence,' he said. 'They want to bribe us into voting to forever be second-class citizens.'

Danai and I gorged on the packets of crisps and flavoured milk that the election men gave to all the children in the township. Our voices rose as we made a song out of the names of the characters on the crisp packets. '*Zsa Zsa the Scarlet, Mama Chompkin, Putzi the Dog, Professor Flubb, Jake the Pirate, Hairy the Hippy.*'

Bishop Muzorewa's voice boomed out across the township. 'Vote for the internal settlement. Vote for an end to war. Vote for schools, for electricity, for a future for you and me.' The next time we heard his voice again was on the radio, when he was announced as the new Prime Minister of our new country, Zimbabwe-Rhodesia.

∾

The war continued in the nine months that we lived in Zimbabwe-Rhodesia, and we did not leave Salisbury. *Sekuru*Lazarus told us that there would be meetings in England to end the war, in a building called Lancaster House, meetings between the guerrillas, and the old white government and the new black and white government. As the year ended, we heard that the talks had ended and there were to be more elections, this time with the guerrillas taking part.

We did not go to Mr Vaswani's shop again, but Juliana brought us news of the schism that had developed between him and his brother. '*Handiti*, you know the brother never really comes to the shop,' *Mainin*'Juliana said, 'but today he was there half the time, and when there were no customers, they were shouting at each other all day.

'The brother said he wants to go to South Africa. We can't just leave, this is our home, your son was born here, said Mr Vaswani. Home nothing, look at Uganda, said his brother. Don't take the boy, leave the boy, said Mr Vaswani, and the brother said, he is coming with us, then Mr Vaswani said, who will take over the shops, and the brother said, he is my son, Sanjiv, not my fault you and Suri can't have children.'

'They should consult healers to open the wife's womb,' my grandmother said and *Sekuru*Lazarus pulled his mouth into a moue and made a sound of disgust and said all Indians should just go back to India if they were so afraid of our independence.

❧

The new elections put Mr Vaswani out of our minds. Everyone said this would mean real independence. My grandmother found herself singing the songs of the moment. '*Na nana ayiyaye Zimbabwe. Africa ayiawo Zimbabwe*' along with Bob Marley became one of the familiar sounds of our house. She was not the only one with Zimbabwe on her lips.

'From tomorrow onwards,' our neighbour on the left informed *Sekuru*Lazarus, 'my business will no longer be called Trymore Panel Beaters, but Zimbabwe Panel Beaters.' Not to be outdone, the man who collected bottles from Mufakose to Glen Norah followed suit, but could only manage Zimbab above the already present Bottle Collectors, unable to fit the rest on the small space of his pushcart.

Throughout the changes visible and invisible that were occurring all around us, my uncle continued *kupaumba*. 'I will never vote for UANC,' he said, 'ZAPU is the party to beat. Joshua Nkomo was there from the beginning. Imagine it, Prime Minister Joshua Nkomo, *hela*!'

Not even *Sekuru*Lazarus swallowed independence with such gasping thirst as my aunt Juliana. She told us of the *gutsaruzhinji* that the guerrillas would bring, the socialism, she said, that meant that there would be no servants and masters, no oppression because everyone would be the same. 'There will be none of this business like you and your madam,' she said to Susan. '*Mu*India had better be careful. If he doesn't watch it, something will happen.'

*Mainin'*Juliana planned all the things that would happen. 'He will have to give us higher wages. We will not work on Saturdays. And with more money, I can do my secretarial.'

'Juliana, I smell a burning pot,' said my grandmother.

We ate our *sadza* and leaf vegetables with charred black meat that night, but we dreamed along with *Mainin'*Juliana and shared *Sekuru*Lazarus's certainty that the Prime Minister would be Joshua Nkomo. Only Susan doubted that the changes would change her life. 'It may well be that there will be this socialism, Juliana,' she said, 'but I can tell you right now that no amount of socialism will make my madam wash her own underwear.'

❧

Two days before the elections, we went back to Mr Vaswani's shop to buy shoes for Danai. 'It's like you have fertiliser in your feet,' *Sekuru*Lazarus said to him. *Mainin'*Juliana had promised us pork pies, and we were looking forward to this treat.

Mr Vaswani's voice stopped us as we left. 'Now, now, Juliana, what is this, where are you going?'

'You said I could leave early today, I have to take the children home,' she said.

'Well, yes, but you look now, there are so wary many customers.'

'I am going,' *Mainin'*Juliana said. 'That was the agreement.'

As she turned to go, Mr Vaswani pulled on the sleeve of her jersey. There was a cry from Mrs Vaswani. The next thing we saw was Mr Vaswani lying on the floor of the shop, blood streaming from his nose, his spectacles beside him, the right eyeglass smashed. Still crying, Mr Vaswani's wife ran out of the shop, a bright pink whirl into the street. She returned just minutes later with a policeman who marched us all to the Charge Office, Mr Vaswani with a handkerchief to his nose, Mrs Vaswani clucking beside him, *Mainin'*Juliana on the policeman's arm and Danai and I following, Danai clutching his shoes to his chest.

The Charge Office was a confused mass of policemen in red-brown shining shoes and khaki uniforms, and people complaining about crime, people accused of crime, and people enquiring about people accused of crime. 'Just sign an admission of guilt, and the whole thing will be over,' the policeman who arrested Juliana said to her in Shona.

The old *Mainin'*Juliana may have done that, but

this new *Mainin'*Juliana was drunk on *gutsaruzhinji*. '*Handina mhosva*,' she shouted. 'I have done no wrong. This is Zimbabwe this, we left Rhodesia behind. I will do it again if I have to.'

'You see how she is threatening me,' said Mr Vaswani. He glowered at Juliana through the still intact left eyeglass. 'Arrest her, arrest her.'

'Arrest me, arrest me,' said *Mainin'*Juliana. 'If you don't, *ndinomuita kanyama kanyama*, you will have to sweep him from these Charge Office floors. Arrest me, arrest me.'

She was arrested.

And this is how *Mainin'*Juliana spent three of Rhodesia's dying days at Salisbury Remand Prison.

❧

*Sekuru*Lazarus was wrong: the new Prime Minister was not Joshua Nkomo after all. After the results were announced, the people on our street crowded into our neighbour's house to watch Prime Minister Robert Mugabe on television. He said it was a time for reconciliation, for turning swords into ploughshares. He said we should reach out our hands in friendship so that black and white could work together to build the new country. Perhaps Mr Vaswani, though neither black nor white, watched the Prime Minister's address too, because two weeks later, he sent Timothy to tell *Mainin*'Juliana that she could have her job back if she wanted it.

'*Ende futi Mu*India thinks he is funny,' she said after her first day back in the shop. 'He is now saying to people that if they steal, he will set me on them. She will beat you like she beat me, he says.'

∾

It took her another three years to achieve her dream, but eventually, *Mainin*'Juliana got a job as a typist at the Ministry of Employment Creation. Mr Vaswani was there with his wife, clapping beside Timothy, *Sekuru*Lazarus, my grandmother, my parents and Danai and me when *Mainin*'Juliana received her secretarial diploma.

'No room for layabouts in this world,' he said again to Danai and me. 'See how hard your auntie works.'

We continued to remind *Mainin*'Juliana about the day she punched Mr Vaswani. Even after she married, and put violence behind her as a staunch pillar of the Anointed Church of the Sacred Lamb, she never quite shook off the reaches of the past, so that even her husband used the incident to cajole their children into behaving. 'Your mother is a boxer,' he said. 'She will deck you like she decked that Indian.'

Mr Vaswani became as much a part of her children's lives as he had been a part of ours. She took them to the shop like she had taken us, only she went as a valued customer the week before the school term. She often came back complaining that Mr Vaswani was getting soft in his old age. 'It is bad management practice to give so many freedoms to employees,' she said.

When she died, Mr Vaswani came to her funeral. He sat with the men of the family while the women whispered his name. When the mourning became too heavy, we laughed at the many ridiculous episodes of her life. We asked one of the family daughters-in-law to imitate the actions of the deceased. Her fist punched the air and the room rang with our laughter as she acted out, without prompting, the right hook that *Mainin'*Juliana gave to Mr Vaswani.

～ The Cracked, Pink Lips
of Rosie's Bridegroom ～

The wedding guests look upon the cracked, pink lips of Rosie's bridegroom. They look at Rosie's own lips that owe their reddish pinkness to artifice, they think, and not disease. Can Rosie see what they see, they wonder, that her newly made husband's sickness screams out its presence from every pore? Disease flourishes in the slipperiness of his tufted hair; it is alive in the darkening skin, in the whites of the eyes whiter than nature intended, in the violently pink-red lips, the blood beneath fighting to erupt through the broken skin.

He smiles often, Rosie's bridegroom. He smiles when a drunken aunt entertains the guests with a dance that, outside this celebration of sanctioned fornication, could be called obscene. He smiles when an uncle based in Manchester, England, calls on the mobile telephone of his son and sends his congratulations across nine thousand kilometres shortened by Vodafone on his end and Econet on the other. His smile broadens as the son tells the master of ceremonies that the uncle pledges two hundred pounds as a wedding gift; the smile becomes broader still when the master of ceremonies announces that the gift is worth two hundred million dollars on Harare's parallel market. He smiles and smiles and smiles and his smile reveals the heightened colour of his gums.

The wedding guests sit in the rented marquee from Rooney's. It is resplendent in the wedding colours chosen by Rosie, cream and buttermilk, with gold to provide the contrast. They chew rice and chicken on the bone and wash it down with mouthfuls of bottled fizzy drinks, beer and an intensive colloquy on Rosie's bridegroom's reputation.

This is his second marriage, everyone knows.

He buried one wife already, even Rosie knows.

What Rosie doesn't know: he also buried two girlfriends, possibly more.

The evidentiary weight of his appearance, circumstantial in isolation, is corroborated not only by the death of one wife and two girlfriends, but by other incidents in the life of Rosie's bridegroom.

For instance: it is known that he was often in the company of Mercy, now deceased, formerly of Glen View Three, notorious Mercy with men from here to Kuwadzana.

Another thing: he drank nightly at the illegal she-been at *Mai*Tatenda's house, with *Mai*Tatenda who has one Tatenda and no *Baba*Tatenda, *Mai*Tatenda who provided her clients with home comforts and then some, *Mai*Tatenda who was seen only last week, just skin and bones, coughing-coughing and shivering in this sweltering December. One doesn't want to be unkind of course, they say, but that is what happens to whores who wrap their legs around men that are not their husbands.

And finally, incontrovertibly: Rosie's bridegroom's car was seen parked outside the house of a prophet who lives in Muhacha Crescent in Warren Park, he of the hands that can drive out the devil Satan who has chosen to appear as an incurable virus in their midst. This prophet has placed an advert in all the newspapers. He responded to that advert, Rosie's new husband, he must have, for his car, the silver Toyota Camry that was always in front of *Mai*Tatenda's house, was seen outside the house of the prophet.

'Is any Sick among You,' the advert says, 'Let him call for the Elders of the Church; and let them Pray over him, Anointing him with Oil in the Name of the Lord. And the Prayer of Faith shall save the sick, JAMES 5:14–15. Jesus of Nazareth Saves,' the advert says. 'Come to have His healing Hands placed upon your Troubled Hearts. All Illnesses Cured. For

Nothing Is Too Hard for Yahweh, GENESIS 18:14.'

There is but one disease that drives men to turn their Toyota Camrys, their Mercedes Benzes, Pajeros, BMWs in the direction of Warren Park. There is only one illness that pushes both the well-wheeled and un-wheeled to seek out the prophet. It is the big disease with the little name, the sickness that no one dies of, the disease whose real name is unspoken, the sickness that speaks its presence through the pink redness of lips, the slipperiness of hair, through the whites of the eyes whiter than nature intended.

They are gifted with prophecy, the wedding guests, they look at Rosie's bridegroom's lips and in them see Rosie's fate. She will die first, of course, for that is the pattern, the woman first, and then the man. The woman first, leaving the man to marry again, to marry another woman who will also die first. They will keen loudly at Rosie's wake; they will fall into each other's arms. Their first tears shed, they will talk of the manner of her death.

In the public spaces they will say: She just fell sick. Just like that, no warning, nothing. She woke up in the morning; she prepared food for the family. Around eleven she said: My head, my head. And by the time she should have cooked the supper, she was gone. So quickly, they will say. No one can comprehend the speed with which it happened. It burdens the heart, they will say. Where have you heard that a person dies from a headache?

But in the dark corners away from the public spaces they will say: *Haiwa*, we knew all along. Her death was there in the bright pink lips of her bridegroom, how far did she think it could go? Remember the first wife, remember Mercy, remember *Mai-*Tatenda, remember the two girlfriends, possibly more? How far did she think it would go?

But that day is still far, it is not here, it is not now. Here and now, the wedding guests clap and cheer and sneer as Rosie dances with her new husband. They pass rice and chicken through their own red-dened mouths, and complain that there is not enough to eat, not enough to drink. The master of ceremonies cries *enko*, *enko*, and the wedding guests dance.

∾ My Cousin-Sister Rambanai ∾

My cousin-sister Rambanai came back from America with two suitcases crammed with too-tight clothes in vivid shades of pink and a new accent. The clothes eventually faded from frequent washes with Cold Power and from hanging in the harshness of the Harare sun, but the accent did not. Her new voice rose and fell in our house as she talked of her life *in the States*, the problems she had juggling her *nine-to-five job* with an *insurance broker* in *down-town Dallas* and her hectic social life, the leaky *faw-cet* in her *duplex*. 'Take this route,' she said, only she pronounced it *rout* instead of *root*. And our house-maid *Sisi*Dessy said to her friend Memory the house-maid from next door that Rambanai sounded just like someone on television.

As the daughter of my father's younger brother, my uncle *Ba'muniniBa'*Thomas, Rambanai was my sister in Shona, my cousin in English, and in

Shonglish, my cousin-sister. Both she and her older brother Thomas lived outside the country but only she came back to bury their father. Instead of coming, Thomas wired seven hundred and fifty pounds through Western Union from Manchester, England where he lived.

'Five years. Five whole years without coming home, not even to bury a father, *heh*,' said my uncle's wife, my uncle's second wife. She was the mother of my twin cousin-brothers Tadiwa and Tadiswa, but not Thomas and Rambanai. 'Is this the behaviour of a responsible son? *Handiye nevanji?* Is it not he, as the new head of the household, who is supposed to be here?'

For all that she complained, it was the money that Thomas sent that enabled the family to bury my uncle in the splendour of the Paradise Peace Casket, a gleaming white coffin with golden handles and a gold frame on the surface into which my aunt put a photograph of my uncle in his University of Leeds graduation cap and gown. When *VateteMai*Mazvita complimented my aunt on the magnificence of the coffin, my aunt blew her nose and swallowed back a sob to say, 'It is a *casket* Vatete, not a coffin. A *casket*.' She covered her face in her handkerchief, and began again to sob softly into its black folds.

Rambanai had not been particularly close to her

father. His forbidding exterior made it impossible for anyone to feel any warmth towards him. When I was a little girl and my uncle's first wife was alive, she had a picture of Jesus on their living room wall. His limpid blue eyes would follow me everywhere. Under the flowing hair, the all-seeing eyes and the pink and blue robes of Jesus were these words: 'I am the silent guest at every meal. I am the silent witness to every action. I am the silent listener to every conversation.' The menace in the words alarmed me and sometimes, after we had visited their house in Mount Pleasant, I woke up screaming that Jesus was in the room and he could hear me breathe. As the picture hung above his favourite seat, I associated the omnipotence of Jesus with *Ba'muniniBa'*Thomas, who sat there without talking, never once laughing in all the time that I knew him, only responding with a grunt when we clapped our hands to him in the traditional way and asked after his health at the beginning of every visit.

The only time he said anything of any length was at the beginning and the end of each term when he sat us down, Rambanai, Thomas, my brother Godi and me, and gave us all a lecture; it was always the same lecture. In his deep slow voice, he called us by name, one by one from the eldest to the youngest.

'Godfrey. Thomas. Matilda. And you, Rambanai.

You must understand, children,' he said, 'the value of education. Every parent hopes that his children will be better off than he was. Every parent looks to education to achieve that hope. Remember, children, the value of education.'

This was the speech he gave, and nothing beyond this, so that when I saw him lying in his coffin during the body viewing on the night that he spent atop the coffee table in the living room, it seemed as though in just a matter of minutes he would raise himself to talk about education before sinking back into his usual silence.

Still, he was Rambanai's father, and I expected that she would be grieved at his passing; a father was a father, after all, even one as unsmiling as *Ba'muniniBa'*Thomas. I did not expect, however, that she would send wails across Immigration and Customs as soon as she saw us. We looked down at her from the observation platform at the airport, with my parents, my aunt and small cousin-brothers we saw her disembark from the aeroplane, cast her face towards us and break into a loud keening that startled the cluster of white visitors waiting in line immediately in front of her. She wept so loudly in the long, slow queue to get her passport stamped that one of the government officials ended up taking her by the arm and fast-tracking her away from the tourists.

In the kitchen, our housemaid *Sisi*Dessy whispered to *VateteMai*Mazvita that Rambanai looked just like her idea of someone who had come from overseas. Having been in America for five years without coming home, she was the star at the funeral; everyone wanted to look at her. She would have given the mourners much to talk about, but she gave them more than they needed. She put her hands to her head. She made as though to jump into the grave. She cried out for her father in a voice hoarse with weeping.

'We all know how hard it is to lose a father, *handiti*,' *VateteMai*Mazvita said, 'but surely, this is too much, *munhu unochemavoka zvine yeyo*. Where have you seen a daughter weeping more than the wife?'

At my uncle's funeral, a special eye was kept on his widow, both to give comfort – and for fear that she might do herself harm. The consensus at my uncle's funeral was that a particularly vigilant eye should also be kept on the daughter, so a younger aunt and I were given the duty of staying with her. In the middle of the night of the day that we buried my uncle, I woke to the sound of a commotion. I looked on the bed and got up when I saw the depressed space where Rambanai's body should have been. I followed the voices outside. I found Rambanai standing in a knot with other women. Their eyes were on my uncle's widow. Two women held her arms as she wailed with her face to the heavens, the Zambia cotton wrapper that was normally tucked securely around her waist folded into a thick rope around her neck. 'I will do it, leave me be. There is no reason now for me to live,' she cried. '*Waenda waenda, waenda murume wangu waenda.*'

'She tried to hang herself off that tree there,' Rambanai said to me as I joined her. She pointed at a peach tree with long thin branches barely able to support the weight of its own fruit.

My aunt was persuaded to go back inside, and after this excessive, if belated, outpouring of grief wept only when the new mourners arrived. Nor did Rambanai equal her own performance at the graveside. It was only later that I understood that Rambanai had been in mourning not only for her father, but also for the death of her American dream.

∾

After the funeral, Rambanai stayed a week, three weeks, one month, five months, eleven. She stayed so long that the question, *vakadii veku*States, moved from *vachadzokera riiniko veku*States to *kuti vachadzokera veku*States. 'Should not your cousin-sister have gone back to Dallas by now?' my boyfriend Jimmy asked me. 'If she stays any longer, she will be here for the *kurova guva* ceremony,' he added, referring to the ceremony that was performed exactly a year after a person's death. I did not answer; I was too busy laughing and trying to stop him from taking my bra off as he drove.

In the eleven months that followed *Ba'munini-Ba'*Thomas's funeral, Rambanai always seemed to be on the verge of departure. She shopped for the many friends she had left behind in America, packed her suitcase, and did the rounds to say her goodbyes. But to hear her tell it, the fates had other plans. Just when she had packed and said her goodbyes, just when we thought now was the moment to take her to the airport, she would tell us about another mix-up with her visa, or a ticketing problem that involved Delta, Air Zimbabwe and American Airways.

'I have confirmed my onward connection from Atlanta to Dallas,' Rambanai said. 'The flight from Jo'burg to Atlanta is sorted. The problem is really with AirZim. From now on, I will only fly SA.'

'Rambanai needs to take three aeroplanes just to get to America,' I heard *VateteMai*Mazvita explain to our housemaid *Sisi*Dessy, and *Sisi*Dessy burnt the meat, I suspect because she got carried away by her contemplation of a journey so long. And when Jimmy said he knew someone who worked at Air Zimbabwe, Rambanai gave a small, tight smile and talked about Dallas.

Rambanai stayed with me and my parents in Mabelreign. 'She wants to stay with her age-mate,' her stepmother said, referring to me, but we knew that she and her stepmother had only talked because of *Ba'muniniBa'*Thomas, and now that he was gone, not even her half-brothers could induce her to spend any time at their home in Mount Pleasant.

We spent the days when I was not at work walking around Harare where Rambanai delighted at the most common sights. 'I want to ride in an emergency taxi,' she said, 'let's take ETs everywhere.' I went along with her even though I preferred to wait for Jimmy to drive me wherever I needed to go. We followed the rituals attendant to riding in ETs, the emergency taxis that were the only reliable form of transport for Harare's commuters. In obedience to the conductors' hectoring commands *garisanai four four* and *ngati-batanidzei tione vabereki nevaberekesi*, we sat buttock to buttock, sixteen people in minibuses that said 'Maximum Passengers: 12'. We collected the ET fares from the passengers behind us, passed them to the passengers in front of us, who passed the money to the passengers in front of them until all the money reached the conductor. Through it all, Rambanai chatted with the drivers and the conductors and any-one else who would listen.

'The public transport is very different in the

States, where I live,' she said. I wanted to sink into my seat, her voice was so loud, but the driver whistled, lowered his volume, and announced to everyone in the car, '*Ava* sister lives in the States.' The people looked at us and a woman with a small child made him sit on her lap so that we could have more space.

With Rambanai, I saw Harare anew. Our feet crushed the fallen jacaranda blooms in Africa Unity Square as hawkers cajoled us to buy their wares. We saw the men at the flower market outside the Meikles Hotel who cried out and tried to persuade random passing men to buy random passing women flowers. We giggled like schoolgirls at the photographers who made people strike old-fashioned poses on the grass of Harare City Gardens. When Rambanai wanted her hair braided, instead of going to Mane Attraction or Nice and Easy or Afro Chic like a normal person, she chose to get her hair done in Mbare township. We spent the day with Rambanai seated on a Zambia wrapper spread on the ground as a woman called Manyara braided her hair, while three other women finished off the ends as Manyara told us about all the government ministers she had slept with in the days she was a prostitute.

'I had them all,' she said as she pulled Rambanai further between her legs so that she could reach the other side of her head. 'There was one businessman, you know the one, *uyu we*tobacco, he had such pink lips you could tell he was sick, but always he said I am an *old madhala, no disease.* But I never went with him which is just as well, *handiti* you know how he died?'

She had us in stitches as she told us how our Minister of Home Affairs had found her in bed with one of the assistant secretaries in the Foreign Affairs Ministry and the latter had almost lost an eye. 'Once they have been here,' she said, and patted her crotch, 'they do not, they cannot go back.'

'*Pakasungwa neutare,*' the women said, and laughed as they clapped hands to each other. Manyara ignored this comment about the iron clasp of her loins and said, 'But these days, *ndinofamba naJesu.* I walk with the Lord now, and all that is behind me. There is no mountain that he cannot move, no task that is too big for him, for nothing is impossible with Jesus.'

She spoke into the silence that followed this sudden change in subject and said, 'But, *takambofara vasikana.*' This recollection of happy times launched her into another tale in which the starring role went to the Governor of the Central Bank and his male appendage which, if Manyara was to be believed, was inversely proportional to the length of his monetary policy statements.

216

The laughter of the finishing women rang out in the afternoon. Naturally merry, Rambanai made them merrier still when she bought them Shake-Shake, the thick traditional beer that I associated with gardeners, miners and other labourers who could not always afford clear beer. I had only seen men drink Shake-Shake, drinking from a shared container in little knots, wiping mouths with the backs of their hands after taking long drags. Shake-Shake was an essentially male drink, I thought, so I was shocked to see women drink it. Rambanai drank too, but I did not like the taste. Manyara diluted the beer with a sweet Cherry Plum soft drink for me, and soon, I was giggling with Rambanai and everyone else. We stayed in Mbare for hours even after Rambanai had finished getting her hair done. Before we left, Manyara said to Rambanai, 'I have a cousin-brother who is willing to do anything, please help him if you can,' and Rambanai gave Manyara her number in America and said she would *definitely* see what she could do.

When we arrived home, my mother shouted and said we should not be walking around at night because people would think we were prostitutes. '*Pakasungwa neutare,*' Rambanai said and patted her crotch, and I laughed until I felt sick and had to run to the bathroom to eject the masticated purplish mess of Shake-Shake and Cherry Plum.

We walked in all the markets of Harare buying curios and small soapstone sculptures. 'I will have to get a bigger suitcase,' Rambanai said. 'Maybe I will leave these wooden bowls behind and take mainly the stuff from the Trading Company. Oh, and the stuff from Mbare too.'

Our housemaid *Sisi*Dessy worshipped Rambanai and could not get enough of her stories. 'America is the land of opportunity, *Sisi*Dessy,' Rambanai told her. 'There you can be anything you want, anything at all. Someone like you can be a housemaid today, and before you know it, you have your own TV show.'

'*Musadaro*,' *Sisi*Dessy said in admiration.

'It is true,' Rambanai said. 'You can be anything at all.'

It was true that Rambanai had developed in areas we had not expected. 'She works for an insurance broker in Dallas, Texas,' I said as I introduced her to my friend Sheila.

'I am also dancer,' Rambanai said.

'But I thought you worked in an office,' said Sheila.

'I also dance.'

'You mean, like a hobby?' asked Sheila.

'No, it is what I am.'

'So you work in an office *and* you dance?'

'I am also a poet.'

'Wow,' said Sheila, and I could see myself going up in her estimation, 'do you have a book, or are you published in magazines?'

'No, not yet, but I am working on it.'

There was silence.

'What about the dance, are you part of a company or some kind of performing group or troupe, you know, like Tumbuka or anything like that?'

'I am working on that too,' said Rambanai. 'I go to a studio four times a week. I will take up flamenco as soon as I get back.'

I overheard *Sisi*Dessy telling her friend Memory the housemaid from next door that in America you could be anything at all that you wanted, you could be a dancer, and a poet all at the same time as you worked in an office. 'If I was in America,' *Sisi*Dessy said, 'I would have my own TV show by now.'

'*Musadaro*,' said Memory.

'It is true,' *Sisi*Dessy said with authority. 'In America, you can be anything you want, anything at all.'

❦

Rambanai stayed so long after the funeral that she was in the crowd of women dressed decorously in colourful Zambia wrappers that sat around the living

219

room when Jimmy's family approached my family to pay the bride wealth for me so that Jimmy and I could be married in the traditional way. At the end of the evening, tempers flared because Jimmy's family thought that my family had been too hard on them.

'This is what you get for marrying a Karanga woman,' Jimmy's friend Tichaona said to him. 'You know they are the most expensive women in the country.' But the thing was done, the balance that could not be given on the night of the marriage would be paid over time, Jimmy and I were married, what remained only was the white wedding.

I could live with Jimmy now, and we moved to our new flat in the Avenues, at the corner of Josiah Chinamano and Third Avenue. Rambanai spent all her time with us, and slowly moved her things in, the tight-tight pink tops and the low-rise jeans, the poncho that she said was cerise but which Jimmy said was bright pink, she moved them in one by one until it seemed almost natural that Jimmy and I should live with her.

'It is convenient here,' she said, 'so close to town.'

'Not so convenient when you are just married and all you want to do to your wife is to . . .' Jimmy said, and I put my hand over his mouth and laughed.

When Rambanai was not with me, she criss-crossed Harare in search of the favourite places from her past. She often came back distraught. 'Can you believe this?' she said upon her return from one such excursion.

I looked up from my magazine, startled to hear the heartbreak in her voice.

'There are flies at the Italian Bakery. Flies, imagine. I was so upset; I could not touch a *thing*. How is it possible that there are so many *flies*?'

It did not seem to me that the fly population of Zimbabwe had increased exponentially since Rambanai's departure. I was about to say something when she continued, 'I went past Avondale Bookshop; it is a stationery shop now. Can you believe they have closed Weng Fu's? He had *the* best spring rolls.'

It seemed to her a personal affront that Weng Fu had gone broke, as though he had done so deliberately to spite her. And it was not only Weng Fu's. The sight of a flea market where there had been a restaurant or ice-cream parlour produced wails of dismay.

'Oh my God, what happened to Ximex Mall?' she said. 'They had *the* best ice cream there. Remember the time I wore that pink top from Edgars with my white jeans from Truworths and my friend Mandi and I met those guys from Saints? No, hang on, they were from Falcon. We had lunch at that restaurant just inside Ximex, on the side of the Post Office and

I had *the* best chicken and apple open sandwiches. There's only that *awful* crap from China in Ximex Mall now, no restaurants, nothing.'

When she tried to track down her old friends and found them fat and fortyish at the age of twenty-seven, she considered this to be a plot against her happiness. 'It is not fair,' she said. 'How can things change so quickly?'

Her Zimbabwe was frozen in 1997, the year she left. Hers had been a country of money to burn, fast guys from Saints and Falcon in fast cars, and party after party, a Zimbabwe without double-digit inflation, without talk of stolen elections. In the absence of the continuity of this life she talked again and again of the old days.

'Do you remember when I first went to Dallas?' she said.

'Yes,' I said, 'and we had the hardest time explaining to *MaiguruMai*Susan that Dallas was a real place but that you would not be meeting Bobby Ewing and Cliff Barnes.'

'Oh, *Dallas*! Remember when Bobby died?'

'Yes, and Pam woke up to find that Bobby's death had been a dream, that the whole season before that had been a dream.'

'I am glad they brought him back,' she said.

'How can you be? They cheated so spectacularly.

222

Why invest all that emotion mourning a person who then comes back from the dead?'

'*Aiwaka*, Matilda,' she said. 'Imagine *Dallas* without Bobby.'

'You kept me up to date on what I missed, do you remember?' I smiled.

She had been at school in town, while I was at boarding school.

'The girls at Chisi thought I was writing to my boyfriend,' she grinned.

'At *my* school, they thought yours were from mine,' I said.

We laughed.

Into the natural pause that followed our laughter she said, 'I am not returning to Dallas.'

I looked up from my ironing.

'There is no way that I can go back to the States,' she blurted. 'I was there illegally. They will not let me back in, I overstayed my visitor's visa.'

'But you were at the university . . .'

'Community college,' she said, and added, 'for only three months.'

'And the job with the insurance broker . . .'

'I worked in a restaurant.'

And the mortgage and the poetry and the dance, I thought, but did not say. And the men; the men, all of them wealthy, all of whom wanted to marry her

223

but there was something wrong with each one.

'I can't go back, but I can't stay here,' she said. 'What would people say? They would say I can't go back, that's what they would say.'

'I know Harare is not Dallas, but is it then so bad?' I asked her gently.

She shook her head.

'I can't be myself here. I want a bigger world. I need to go back. But I cannot use my passport. I'll show you, it has been endorsed.' She showed me the passport and I saw the words *May not be granted leave to enter* stamped like angry welts on a face.

'What will I do?' she said as she wept into her hands. 'It is hard, so hard. Everything is so hard.'

'We have to help her,' I said to Jimmy when he came home that evening.

'Help her what?' Jimmy said. 'We should help her find a job.'

The next morning, he read aloud to her the few vacancies that appeared in the newspaper. 'I want a bigger world,' she said as she put marmalade on her toast. 'Bigger world *yekutengesa ma*hamburger,' Jimmy said, when she was out of hearing, and I hushed him for fear that she would hear.

'*Kana ada zvekutsava*, there is always Macheso,' he said. 'She can be one of his backup dancers if she wants to dance. Or if she wants to be Paul Mkondo, there are insurance companies here too.'

He picked up his keys to go to work and sang. '*Itai penny penny vakomana ndatambura. Vakomana urombo uroyi. Kana usina mari hauna shamwari.*' It was only after the door closed behind him that I realised that he was singing the song from the old Paul Mkondo insurance programme on Radio 2.

❧

The burden of the truth off her shoulders, Rambanai sang along to Boyz II Men on her disc-man, clogged up the bathtub drain with the artificial hair from her weave, and told me her plans for our money. 'America is a non-starter,' she said cheerfully. 'They will never give me a visa now. I will go to London. At least we don't need visas for England, being in the Commonwealth. In England, I can get an office job. I will continue my dancing. Or maybe acting, I have always wanted to be an actress. I will get a proper job, go to school at night. I will do something.'

'But your passport was endorsed . . .'

She waved away the endorsement as if it were of no consequence.

'Exactly. I can't go as me; they have records, you know. I need another passport in another name. That's what lots of people do when they have been deported, they just get new passports.'

'*Mainini*, new passports don't grow on trees,' said Jimmy.

'Exactly,' beamed Rambanai, 'and that is why you have to help me get another one.'

'Oh, and I will need a new name,' she added. 'There is a record on me now. I can choose any name I like. Tamera, Chantal, Michelle. I know, I will choose a Ndex name. They have some really cool names. Nonhlanhla. Busisiwe. Sihle. Gugulethu. I know, Langelihle, that means beautiful day. You can just call me Langa for short. I can be Ndebele. Oh, I could even be a Ndebele princess.'

'But you are not Ndebele,' I said.

She went on as though I had not spoken, 'It will be so cool to be Ndex, you know, with the whole Zulu connection. You know Oprah Winfrey is part Zulu, right?'

'*Mainini*, I don't know what they are telling you in America, but from what I remember of my history, no Zulus were taken to America as slaves,' said Jimmy.

'You don't even *speak* Ndebele,' I said.

'I'm sure there are lots of Ndebele people who don't speak the language,' she said. 'I can be one of them! What would they know about it in England?'

'But your certificates,' I said in dismay, 'how will you get a job without your O level and A level certificates? Those are in your own name.'

'I will just focus on my dance,' she said. 'And maybe acting, I have always wanted to be an actress. You remember how I used to act at school.'

In my mind, together with Rambanai as a pregnant Mary in the nativity play in which she appeared when she was eleven, I also saw *Ba'munini-Ba'*Thomas spinning and spinning in his Paradise Peace Casket as he talked in his resonant voice about the value of education.

∾

Jimmy would not give her money, but I brought him round in the end. A new, unendorsed passport in another name would not be cheap. We sold some shares that Jimmy's father had left him. We postponed buying a new fridge and stove for our flat. These sacrifices caused some strain between Jimmy and me, and I had to make Rambanai promise to send us back our money as soon as she sorted herself out. 'I will send it within a month of arriving,' she said. 'You can trust me, you'll see.'

We spent interminable days waiting for a new birth certificate, before we waited for a new ID card, and then finally, a new passport. Our mission began in Makombe Building where Rambanai procured the first proof of her new existence in the form of a Republic of Zimbabwe birth certificate. We waited

227

among infants crying at their mothers' exposed breasts and we listened to the voices of the desperate.

'I have travelled all this way, please just help me, *mukuwasha*.'

'*Imi ambuya*, there is nothing we can do if you do not produce the child. How do we know the child exists if we do not see it?'

'What would the point of lying about a non-existent child? It is not as though I get anything from the government. Why would I say I have a child when I don't?'

'If you have this child, why not just bring it?'

'*Nhai mukuwasha, kana murimi*, how can I possibly bring a child to wait in this heat?'

The man pointed at the red-faced babies crying in the heat. 'So are these not babies? What is so special about yours that you cannot bring it here? *Makazvara chidhoma*?'

The babies wailed, their mothers pulled them to their breasts and sat down on the chairs and on the ground to feed them and the babies sucked down the smell from a nearby broken sewer with their mother's milk.

We did not wait long among the new mothers; we were soon ushered into one of the offices. The man assisting us was all smiles as he said, 'Have you prepared my parcel?' When Rambanai handed him an

228

envelope, he opened it, took out the wad of notes, stuck his finger to his tongue and with an expert hand counted out the money. He made a phone call. While he asked Rambanai about America, a young man came with an envelope which contained the birth certificate of Langelihle Chantal Ndhlukula, born on the date Rambanai had dictated, which was two years after the year of her real birthday. 'I have always wanted to be born in December,' Rambanai said. 'This way, I can be a Capricorn. And look, I won't turn thirty for at least five years.'

This was only the first part; she needed a new ID, and a similarly stuffed envelope secured her a metal ID in record time. That river crossed, we headed towards the grey bungalow which housed the Passport Office, and waited outside Window Number 6 to process the application. The place was crawling with street kids who acted as place holders in the queues while people slept, ate or relieved themselves, and who also offered the benefits of their experience to the waiting applicants. A boy no older than twelve shouted out instructions as more people joined the queue.

'Make sure you have everything. Long birth certificate, ID, father's ID, mother's ID, mother's and father's death certificate if deceased, marriage certificate if married, husband's ID if married, one passport form, two photographs. Hands must be clean for the fingerprints.'

'*Nhai mwananagu*,' a troubled elderly woman asked him, 'they surely can't want to see the father's ID. Does that apply even to us, old as we are?'

'There is no one without a father,' the boy said. To another woman he said, 'As for you, sister, I can tell you right away that you are wasting your time. They won't accept your photos; you need to show your ears.'

As Rambanai and I got nearer to Window Number 6, we heard a dreadlocked man shouting, 'But it is my religion, this is my religion.' The woman he shouted at was protected from his anger by a metal grille. 'Yes, yes,' she said and bit into a biscuit, 'it may well be your religion, but that has nothing to do with your passport. We do not allow dreadlocks.' To the woman who approached her after the dreadlocked man, she said, '*Mototorwa dzimwe* sister, you are smiling in these pictures. You cannot smile in your passport photo.'

The message spread through the queue. No dreadlocks, artificial hair or any other headgear, no smiling pictures. 'Why would you be smiling for a passport photo?' the street kid said with contempt in the direction of the departing smiler, and to the dreadlocked man, 'As for you, get a haircut.'

When our turn came, we gave the name of the woman who had been referred to us. She smiled as she said to us, 'Why are you in this dreadful queue, you should have come round the entrance.' We found our way to the hallowed sanctuary of Office 56, where, in exchange for another envelope, Rambanai was fingerprinted and documented. Thus it went on; in exchange for yet another envelope, someone in Mkwati Building got her police clearance, and a week later, the passport arrived, green and pristine and smelling of new opportunities. Rambanai kissed it when she saw it. She kissed Jimmy too, and I had to nudge him in the back to get him to let go.

'I will not forget you,' she said. 'You must *definitely* stay with me if you ever visit England. I will repay every cent.' Ten months after she was supposed to have left for Dallas, Texas, we took Rambanai on another round of goodbyes. We took her to the airport with her suitcase full of sculptures and cloths from the Trading Company. We fought through a crowd of white-garmented people praying over a departing family. 'Let them go in your name, Jehovah. Guide them through the perils of immigration. Remove the thoughts of Satan from those who would deport them.' And though she did not join the prayer, I know that Rambanai's heart was thud-thud-thudding under her tight-fitting pink shirt as she waved to us and walked across to board the British Airways flight to London.

∾

She called to say she had arrived, but as Jimmy and I did not have a landline at the flat, the phone call was to my mother who passed it on to me. Even after I got a mobile phone and passed the number to my mother and to my aunt to give to Rambanai if she called again, she did not call. I expected daily that I would get a letter or a postcard with Buckingham Palace on it, but there was no word. And there was no money.

I even subjected myself to my aunt's weekly prayer meetings in Mount Pleasant to see if she had heard from Rambanai. I looked for her name on ZimUpdate and ZimUnite and other websites for homesick Zimbabweans abroad until I remembered that she had changed her name and looked for her in her new identity. But there was nothing, only to be expected, I told myself, because Langelihle Chantal Ndhlukula had no history. There would be no one looking for her because she was nowhere, she was nothing.

I did not see Rambanai on the Internet, but memories of her came to me in Harare, in all the places we had visited. I even went to Mbare to get my hair done, but it was not as it had been. Manyara was too sick to talk much, progress was slow as she hacked a cough into my hair as she plaited it. 'Do you know, your cousin-sister promised to do something for my cousin-brother?' Manyara said. I promised that I would call Rambanai and do what I could, and I took down Manyara's number. I paid her all her money even though she had not finished doing my hair and instead of going back the next day, I undid it. I saw her about a year later at the Chicken Inn on Inez Terrace. 'Do you remember me?' she said and I knew her instantly even though she was thin in the face and her lips were cracked and pink. I recognised her but I did not want to talk about Rambanai so I pretended that she had mistaken me for someone else.

Exactly one year after Rambanai caught her flight to London, the British embassy imposed visa restrictions on Zimbabweans. Two and a half years after that, Jimmy and I decided to join the three million who had left the country. It was an economic decision, we explained to everyone who asked, it is an economic decision, we said to ourselves, but in our hearts, we knew that leaving our families was the only way to save our marriage. The time had come for our families to expect something, translucent ears, a bulging stomach, an aversion to strong scents, anything that could be evidence of a baby on the way.

'Is she spitting-spitting, or frowning-frowning yet,' they asked, and sent emissaries to enquire whether there was anything showing. We had tried, but nothing was happening, or happening quickly enough, and I could no longer bear the looks and the whispered conversations at funerals that stopped as soon as I entered the room. We thought of England then, and my thoughts turned to Rambanai.

'Rambanai is somewhere in Birmingham,' her brother Thomas said the first time I called him. Then she was in Newcastle, then Leicester, then back in London. Our emails bounced into empty air, our phone calls went unanswered.

In the end, we got our visas the same way Rambanai had got her passport, we used the Harare way – someone knew someone in the British embassy with whom we exchanged envelopes stuffed with cash. I gave up teaching and Jimmy engineering to be in England, where the curse of the green passport condemned us to work in the unlit corners of England's health care system, in care homes where we took out the frustrations of our existence by visiting little cruelties on geriatric patients. I thought often of *Ba'muniniBa*'Thomas who had believed that education would guarantee our future.

Even as my ears took in the sounds of London, the cries to *help the homeless help themselves, buy the Big*

Issue, the preacher at Oxford Street station who spoke of hell and damnation in such soft tones he may as well have been advertising a weekend at a holiday camp, the thundering sound of the train between underground stations, I listened to my heart as it spoke of Rambanai. Then I saw her, on a biting February morning on an escalator at Liverpool Street station when my frozen thoughts were on the care home job that awaited me at the end of the Jubilee line. She was on an escalator going in the opposite direction, her coat bright pink among the hues of London's black-clad. The joy in my voice was sincere as I called out her name. She looked up and beamed like I was the very person she expected to see sliding up the escalator at Liverpool Street.

'Hey, Matilda,' she cried, and tried to reach out across the space between the escalators. I reached out too and we clung to the edges of the moving stairs, our hands passing without meeting.

We laughed at our failure.

'I'll wait for you at the top,' I said to her.

'I'm running late and I have to catch my train, yeah,' she shouted, 'but make sure you call me, all right? Call me, yeah? Tonight, yeah?'

On that escalator at Liverpool Street station, under the gimlet stares of the suited ones, all I could say was a faint *okay* that I am not sure reached her.

Only as I watched her glide down past the framed adverts for *Queen* the musical and the latest Harry Potter did it occur to me that I did not have her phone number. By this time, she had disappeared from my view and I imagined her, a chameleon in pink, pushing her way among the dark shapes on the platform, fighting to get onto the train in the rush hour.

❧ The Negotiated Settlement ❧

Thulani did not immediately notice the darkness. Only when he was in the house and reached for the wall switch in the entrance corridor to produce an empty click did he realise that there was no electricity. Load shedding. He walked to the kitchen, singing snatches of Oliver Mtukudzi, '*Zvimwe hazvibvunzwi, zvimwe hazvibvunzweiwe.*'

After all these years in Harare, his Ndebele tongue still couldn't get around the Shona *zv* and *nzw* sounds. It probably never would. He abandoned singing, and hummed as he groped for a candle where they kept them above the fridge. He lit one and opened the microwave oven. *Isitshwala* and stewed meat and leaf vegetables again. He had to unpeel the skin from the *isitshwala* to eat it. It had the smoky taste of food cooked over an open fire. The meat was cold and the vegetables clammy in his mouth. He washed his meal down with the remaining half-pint of Pilsener that he had smuggled out of the Mannenberg. It was warm from being cradled between his legs on the drive home.

'Dinner by candlelight,' he said.

He found this funnier than it was, and chuckled. He hummed more Oliver as he ate. Eleven mouthfuls later, the candle in his hand cast his shadow against the wall as he walked into the bedroom. The candlelight flickered over the outlined shape of his sleeping wife. He removed his shirt and trousers, leaving them in a heap on the floor and got into bed. His wife shifted in her sleep towards his side of the bed. Thulani felt a stir of desire, but it was a flash only, it died as quickly as it rose. He lay back and tried to recapture his earlier ebullience. What was that joke Themba had told again? He should have been more serious with Themba, it looked like he was really going to marry that woman.

'You do not need to do this,' he had said to him, but Themba had only laughed and said vague things about settling down. He should have been firmer, he should have told him that settling down was simply settling, that he was giving permission to fate to stifle him and kill all his freedom.

'There's the padlock, see.'

He struggled to remember where those words came from. He gave up the effort, and it came back

240

to him. Arabella, showing off her wedding ring after the remarriage to that poor bastard, Jude Fawley. He hadn't thought about *Jude the Obscure* since the last time he read it, almost nineteen years ago, when he had had to cram it for a literature exam. Another passage came to him now as he tried to find sleep: 'Take her all together, limb by limb, she's not such a bad-looking piece – particular by candlelight.'

He got up. His wife slept on. Picking up his discarded clothes, he moved into the lounge and dressed himself again. In the darkness, he stretched out on the three-seat sofa. Just after they had bought it six years ago, he had tried to make love to Vheneka on this sofa, anything to kill the monotony, but she had said, no, no, the kids, and he had not tried again.

He went over to the bookshelf, and got down his secret stash of cigarettes. He lit one and lay back on the sofa. His thoughts drifted as he smoked. He saw in his mind's eye his wife's naked body, the breasts, the protruding stomach, the scar of Nkosana's Caesarean.

'First you undo me this scar, then we can talk about divorce,' she had said, when three years ago, in a moment of unbearable suffocation he had asked for his freedom. He had not talked about it again.

Had he really wanted to leave? There seemed nothing active about his life now. He no longer desired her, no longer thought about returning home, surprising her, no longer sought her first thing in the morning. He remembered how beautiful she had been to him once, and even now, she could surprise him sometimes, when unexpected, the scent of her came to disturb him, and she turned, and laughed, and he saw, beneath the puffed cheeks and strange hairstyle of the moment, the girl he had seen at the Students' Union.

He had wooed her on walks to Avondale, with Chinese food and combo-packs from Chicken Inn. Flowers from Interflora and movies at Kine 600. He had endured the endless ragging of his Bulawayo friends who mocked him for falling for a Shona chick, but even they had to admit that she was so beautiful she could have been Ndebele. On the night of her twentieth birthday, he had taken her to Gabrielle's, but she wanted to go to the Manchurian. The forty dollars he had saved for this night felt suddenly light in his pocket and when the bill came, his insides turned to water.

He would leave his ID card, he had resolved, and was just about to go over to talk to the waiter when she put her hand on his.

'We can share the cost,' she said. He had protested of course, but not too much, and eventually had given in. They had held hands all the way back to the university, and later, in Manfred Hodson Hall, in the room he shared on P corridor with Xholisa Bhebhe, on a narrow bed sagging from the sex of all the students that had come before them, they conceived their first child.

He had not meant to marry at twenty-one, but that first pregnancy had left him with no other honourable option. The consolation had been the sex. He had enjoyed feeling superior when he heard his fellow-students' desperate searches for sex. Not for him the prowls through the townships, looking for easy lays that opened their legs at the flash of a university student identity card; or the hours drinking at the Terraskane Hotel to summon the courage needed to approach a woman and take her to the Welcome Lodge opposite, where 'resting for thirty minutes' was sixty dollars and 'resting for an hour' was a hundred. Thulani had been spared this search. He had a woman with whom he could have endless legal sex.

Now, when he wants sex, he does not always go to his wife. He had had a girlfriend once, but his wife had found out; that was a time in his life that he did not think about, could not afford to think about. Even as he thought this, another thought came; the child is probably eleven. There is an eleven-year-old child with my blood in him or her. There is a child that is part of me out there. He pushed the thought from his mind.

Some of his friends had what they called small

houses. He had never tried such an arrangement; small-house women expected as much money and attention as the real wives. The thought of not one, but two women each expecting everything from him, each treating him with that special brand of passive aggression that was fed into women with their mother's milk, was enough to make him give up sex altogether.

He had decided to avoid such permanent arrangements, settling instead for occasional encounters. At the Law Society Summer School, with a willing colleague, preferably one who was married herself, and could console herself with the knowledge that she was doing only what her husband was doing.

Thulani lit another cigarette and smiled as he thought that the crisis in the country had become a boon industry for lawyers. They held conferences at Troutbeck Inn and Leopard Rock, holiday resorts where no tourists came, but only the NGO officials, constitutional law experts and human rights lawyers who pontificated on what they called the appalling and unacceptable and ever-deteriorating human rights situation in the country. Before the elections, they held seminars on creating the right space for democratic transition, and after the elections, they hosted conferences at which they gave post-mortems. And the donor money rolled in, real money, dollars and pounds and euros.

After they had analysed the lack of democratic space and inveighed against the partisan actions of the police, they had sex. Thulani had been with Estella Mhango at the last conference; she had been three years behind him in school. She had failed constitutional law twice but was now styling herself a constitutional law expert and human rights activist.

The evening with Estella had been unsatisfactory enough not to be repeated. Funny, he thought, what was it with really beautiful women? There was something wooden about them, like they had been told so often that they were beautiful that they did not seem to feel the need to make an effort. Not Vheneka, though. She had never been like that. At least, not at first.

He did not trouble to find excuses for cheating on Vheneka. There seemed to be something obscene about sex with her, as though he was doing it with a relative. What added to the frisson was that he still felt the occasional flicker of desire. If he was to be honest with himself, it was not her that he desired, but the sex itself. In the dark, she could have been any woman. And this is what Themba wanted, this padlocked life. Thulani was suddenly tired. He stretched and yawned.

He slept and dreamed of Oliver.

❧

When Vheneka woke the next morning, she made straight for the living room. Thulani was still asleep. She left him, showered, and with their maid, dressed and fed the children. She returned to the living room. Thulani slept on. He had drool coming out of the corner of his mouth. She shook him awake, and without waiting for him to rouse himself fully, she said, 'How could you come home so late? I tried to call you, but your phone was switched off.'

He mumbled, and she repeated herself.

'The battery was low,' he said.

He yawned. She could see the dark filling of a molar at the back of his mouth. He closed his eyes again. She was suddenly angry, and fought to control herself as she said, 'How can you keep coming home at this time? What would happen if I also start coming home late every night? Who would help the children with their homework?'

She could feel her voice rising into harsh ugliness but she could not prevent it. 'And that tap in the yard has been broken for a long time now, it is still leaking and I keep asking you to get someone to fix it but you never do.'

'Well, why don't you sort it out then?'

'Why should I do everything around here?'

'I said I would fix it.'

'Promises. That's all you are good for.'

He got up to walk to the bathroom. As he closed the door she said, 'That's right, walk away, like you always do.'

Later, as she drove the children to school, she thought how worn the grooves were along which they moved their quarrels. She could feel herself saying all the clichéd phrases of a thousand injured women before her, but she could never stop herself. She wanted to make it specific to her and him, to them, Vheneka and Thulani, but it all came down to the same thing, promises not kept and not made. Words not said, embraces not given. Their quarrels were never resolved. They were simply postponed to another day. And they were never about what was wrong.

As she drove away from the children's school, she found herself thinking, as she had so often before, that even her name was not her own. Vheneka Dhlamini, Mrs Dhlamini to her colleagues. Her new name, her Ndebele name and her fluency in her husband's language were not enough to deceive native Ndebele speakers, but it was enough for some of her Shona colleagues to treat her differently. Just last week, she had heard the history teacher ask the biology teacher why it was that the Ministry was giving these Ndebele teachers jobs in Harare when there were schools in Bulawayo.

As she turned into Prince Edward, Vheneka shook off these thoughts and focused instead on the memory of the Vheneka Chogugudza who had played centre at netball and had grown into a woman aware of the power of her own beauty, the way it unsettled the men around her. There had not been many men, just Patrick, before he went to Poland to study, and then Thulani.

She smiled as she remembered those early days, when they had sometimes spent whole mornings and afternoons in bed, tasting each other. There had been dreams. Little things to hope for, aspire towards. Education for their children, professional success, two family cars. Travel to South Africa, maybe even to England. Small, small things burned in the flames of inflation.

After the pregnancy with Nobuhle, there was only one thing to be done. She knew that what she felt for him was not what he felt for her. She wanted only him. He had not been the first, but he was the last. She had not been his first, and she certainly knew she was not the last.

Nobuhle had died at five years, of meningitis said the doctors, witchcraft said hers and Thulani's mothers. That was the beginning, she thinks. She tottered, but did not fall. Then the blow that had felled her: Thulani had made another woman pregnant. The woman had come to her school, she loved Thulani, she had said, and he loved her. There was nothing that could be done, she was going to have his child. She was four months pregnant she had said. Due at Christmas. And Nobuhle was dead.

Thulani stayed. She had not asked him, but he did. He had said nothing about the other child. She had asked no questions. Part of her knew that he remained for reasons more complicated than love. She had Busisiwe and Nkosana after that, but like a missing tooth that is present even in its absence, Nobuhle remained.

She knew, throughout the years, that Thulani had other women; she had seen the evidence. After his last Law Society conference, she had found a packet of condoms in his jacket. It had been opened. Two were missing. There was ice around her stomach, but her only coherent thought was to wonder whether both condoms had been used on the same occasion.

And after that, her revenge – Peter Kapuya, the trainee teacher straight from Belvedere Teachers' College. She seduced him in her car as she drove him home after a late staff meeting to discuss a strike. She had resented him, this stranger, with his unfamiliar intrusion, but the memory of the missing condoms spurred her on. That night, for the first time in months she had made the first move towards Thulani.

As Vheneka checked her mirror before driving into the school, she caught her reflection. 'To look so antique and me only thirty-five,' she said. She was suddenly frightened as she imagined another fifteen years of this.

Thulani had once asked for a divorce.

She had felt then a wave of rage so sharp it threatened to cut her sanity, but she had forced herself to speak slowly, calmly. In his language she had told him, 'First you undo me this scar, then you unlearn me this language. After that, you can come back and we can talk about divorce.'

He had said nothing more after that. Sometimes she thought that *she* should leave *him*, but the fear of being alone hits her. She has nothing beyond him, beyond her family; the job she loved has deserted her. She can no longer escape to her great love, can no longer explore plot and plot devices in *The Mayor of Casterbridge*, find pleasure in explaining iambic pentameter. The girls she teaches are not interested. And who can blame them? How will Eliot and Pinter and Golding get them a fast buck? What guarantees do Achebe and Marechera and Dangarembga offer? They want the new subjects, computer science, accounts, economics, management of business. They want to find a way to London now, to act on *Studio 263*, to enter beauty pageants.

As she walked away from her car, she heard someone calling out to her. She turned. It was Thulani. She looked from him to his car, which he had parked outside the school gate.

'You followed me,' she said. The words sounded like an accusation.

'I don't have time for this,' she said.

'This is not about us,' he said. There was something in his voice, but before she could speak, her mobile phone rang from her handbag.

'Let it ring,' he said.

She looked from him to the bag, and knew from his face that nothing was right.

'I followed you, your brother called just after you left, but I wanted to tell you myself.'

The children, she thought, the children. But they were safe, they were in school, she had taken them there herself.

'It is your mother,' he said. 'There was nothing anyone could do. Your brother said she just collapsed, and that was it.'

The phone rang again.

'Leave it,' he said again.

'But the people, all the relatives, friends, they will want to say . . . to know the arrangements,' she said.

'And the school,' she added, 'I can't go to class now. I have to tell Mrs Muza.'

He walked with her to the headmistress's office where the message was given and understood. As they walked back across the school quadrangle, the bell rang for morning lessons. They were caught in a sea of laughing girls in green and white uniforms running to their classrooms. Their voices faded as Thulani and Vheneka walked to the car park.

The phone rang again as they neared the car. She reached inside her bag for it, and he caught her hand. 'I am sorry for your loss,' he said, in the most formal expression of condolence that Shona allowed.

Why doesn't he hold me, she thought, why does he say the words of a stranger, why, but even before she had completed the thought, he had taken her other hand. She was afraid to cry because she knew, when it came, she would not stop. Then she was in his arms and he was holding her and he held on to her as they walked to the gate. They left her car behind and drove back home in his. On the way, they talked about calling the funeral home and about all the other things, large and small, that needed to be done.

∾ Midnight at the Hotel California ∾

It is hard to remember that there was ever a time when you could buy a half-dozen eggs, a packet of Colcolm sausages, two loaves of bread, a packet of Tanganda tea and still have change from a ten dollar note for two Castle lagers and a packet of Everest. I was thinking of those days as I walked from Mbare to Tynwald today. I had gone to Mbare to collect my car, but my mechanic Lovemore had not finished with it.

A couple more days, *m'dhara*, he said.

I had to contend with that. Shaky called while I was in Mbare and said that he knew someone who knew someone who could get me a good deal on fifty litres of petrol. It is a super deal, *m'dhara*, he said, it is only valid today, take it or leave it.

I could not leave it; this was the only thing in my pipeline. Just ten days ago, I had had to suspend another deal – some moron thought he was doing me the world's greatest favour by offering me nine hundred billion for a four-stroke diesel generator. He actually expected that I would smile and say *Jesu wangu*, but I said, forget it, there can be no deal for such a low price, and he said, you will not be able sell it for more, and I said, I would rather hang on to it in that case, *simbi haiore, m'dhara, uye haidyi sadza*.

These were thin times in the Gumbo household with the wife pulling faces, and in the small house the girlfriend was suddenly too busy to see me. So when Shaky's super take-it-or-leave-it fuel deal came up, I set off at once. There was no transport to be found, and I had to walk all the way from Mbare to Tynwald.

My immediate thought when I saw the fellow I was supposed to meet was that he was high on something. I am Clever by name and Clever by nature, ha, ha, ha, he said, and ha, ha, ha, I said, now how much do you want for it? He pushed back dreadlocks from his forehead and said he wanted half a billion. You are dreaming, I thought to myself, and pulled out one of the drinking straws that I carried in my battered Old Mutual briefcase. I put the straw into the barrel, sucked at it to draw some of the fluid into my mouth, which was just as well because there was definitely something else mixed in with the petrol. I spat it out, hoping that it was only water and not urine – urine is preferred by the more unscrupulous because it is the same colour as petrol.

I know nothing about it, *m'dhara*, I am just the middleman, said Clever by name and Clever by nature. I was too tired to argue, it did not matter who was to blame, because the long and short of it was that I had nothing for my trouble, and to add to this, I now had to walk all the way back to town.

I tried to call Shaky. The number you have dialled is not available at the moment, said the electronic Econet voice, please try again later. I called his Telecel and NetOne numbers, same message different voices. My mood soured even further as I trudged past an ostentatious private school in Tynwald that everyone said was run by a retired army general.

As I walked, I thought about following up on another fuel lead that another contact had told me about. Here is how it works: there are these new farmers who get fuel at give-away bottom dollar everything-must-go preferential government prices. The government will throw anything at the new farmers to make them produce: cheap fuel, free tractors, free seed, free fertiliser – even free labourers; they were using prisoners on farms at one time. Pity they can't throw in a bit of free motivation because the thing about the new farmers is that they don't use the cheap fuel for their free tractors; instead, they sell both tractors and fuel to people like me, and people like me sell them on to the vast majority of the unconnected non-preferential-rate-getting masses that can only get fuel on the black market.

It's against the law, of course, this black market thing, but they may as well arrest every living person between the Limpopo and the Zambezi and have done with it. This is the new Zimbabwe, where everyone is a criminal. One of my best customers, His Worship, Mr Mafa, is a regional magistrate for Harare, and another, the Right Reverend Malema, is a stalwart of the Anointed Church of the Sacred Lamb. The last time I sold diesel to His Worship, he paid off a little of what he owed me in tomatoes – his office at Rotten Row is crammed with the vegetables he grows on a small plot of land along the Bulawayo Road at the edge of which the City of Harare has placed large rusting signs that say NO CULTIVA-TION: TRESPASSERS WILL BE PROSECUTED.

Unlike those poor sods who have found that their cherished degrees are useless in this new economy, I at least have not fallen too far off my track. I am using the skills I honed as an insurance man in the eighties and nineties. My ex-brother-in-law used to say I could sell dental floss to his mother-in-law – the woman had fewer teeth than a hen.

It is not just fuel either. I am what you might call an all-commodity broker: if it can be bought, it can be sold, and if it can be sold, I am your man. I have bought and resold computers that the President donated to rural schoolchildren in Chipinge during the last election campaign – they don't need them after all, their schools have no electricity. I have sold reconditioned cars from Japan and Singapore, flat-screen televisions from Dubai, sugar and salt and children's toys from South Africa. I have even sold water-purifying chemicals from Malaysia to the City Council of Kwekwe. All goods processed, no questions asked. No guarantees, no returns, no refunds. No wire transfers, no credit cards – as the sign at the Why Not Hotel, Esigodini says, Mr Credit Was Killed By Mr Cash.

Last year, I sold my biggest item yet: a John Deere combine harvester which came down to me from some poor white bastard who had been compelled to donate his land for redistribution by the magnanimous Comrades. When the Comrades redistribute the land, they also make sure to redistribute any crops on the land, all machinery, any furniture, plates, knives and forks, and any whisky that might be in the house.

So that's how a lucky Comrade got a free combine harvester and having no need for it in urban Warren Park, he sold it to me for only one and a half trillion. I sold it for at least a hundred times that amount, got

259

US dollars too, which I sold on at a healthy profit, and that is how I was able to buy a third-hand RAV4 for the wife, pay three lots of school fees in one go and get the girlfriend a four-day weekend at Vic Falls and all the one hundred per cent human hair (made in Taiwan) that she could buy.

I was musing on all these deals as I crossed the field that divides Tynwald from Ashdown Park and walked to the corner of Eves and Ashdown Drive. I thought I might get a lift to town here. I bought an Everest from a vendor who had set up a stall at the corner. As I lit my cigarette, I was almost run over by a huge silver Prado that screeched to a halt beside me. The driver jumped out leaving his door open, and bought a couple of cigarettes from the vendor.

I was about to say something to him when I was distracted by the music coming from his car. I would know that riff even in the pits of hell. The Eagles. 'Hotel California'. The music poured from his car and into Ashdown Drive. My rage went away in an instant. I laughed hard. The young man and the street vendor looked at me. They were joined in their curiosity by three men who had been waiting for transport to town. It is not every day a man goes mad at the corner of Eves and Ashdown Drive. Their baffled faces made me laugh harder, and buckled by the strength of my laughter, I doubled over.

Ko ndeipi blaz? the Prado driver asked.

You will not believe me if I tell you, I said.

Try me, he said.

Now here was an opportunity.

I will only tell you if you give me a lift to town, I said. I nodded towards the other three. Give all of us a lift and I will tell you the best story you have heard your whole life.

One *mita* each, he said.

I summoned the three who clambered into the car. I got into the passenger seat. We handed over a million dollars each to our driver and drove off in the final blasts of the Eagles. As we drove down Harare Drive, I told them about the time, back in the swinging nineties, when Zimbabwe was still Zimbabwe and I had spent a night at the Hotel California.

❧

My hero as a child had been Paul Mkondo; that song from his money programme had been the theme song of my youth. He was everything I wanted to be, and so it was only natural that I associated the insurance business with money, and sought to make my fortune in that line. As an insurance salesman, I was successful because I had hit on the bright idea of sticking mainly to the small towns that most salesmen avoided. Not for me Harare and Bulawayo, or Gweru and Kwekwe, Mutare and even extended villages disguised as towns like Marondera. There were any dozen insurance sellers here. I frequently turned my Datsun Bluebird towards the small mining areas and tiny towns, not quite going to the rural areas, but skirting them, Kamativi and Karoi, Esigodini and Hwange.

I made a surprisingly steady sale; you would be amazed at the number of miners and small-town teachers in those days that had money stashed under pillowcases, and whom I managed to persuade to give a little of it to insurance. I sold protection in a suitcase, with just a signature on the dotted line, I secured futures, one copy for you, and two for the file. There was another bonus, the many lonely housewives I encountered. And there was nothing like driving the long lonely stretches of road with nothing but myself for company and the Bhundu Boys on the stereo.

On one such occasion, at about seven in the evening, I came to Kamativi. I thought I would surprise Mabel, one of my women. I had not seen her since I last came to Kamativi four months before this when her husband had been at his mine job. A bed for the night, and, if I knew Mabel, a half night of pleasure awaited me, and I was filled with anticipation. I scrounged around to see what I could bring

262

her, and managed to find two warm bottles of lager in the boot of the Datsun. My condoms were in my briefcase as usual and I carried everything to the house, together with a couple of newspapers. That would have to do, and, parking my car, I made my way towards the house.

Even before I could knock, there was her husband, short in stature but large in suspicion. And behind him, Mabel, a tall woman, who seemed suddenly reduced, simpering and smiling and looking everywhere but at me. A woman with half a brain would have said I was an uncle, or a cousin, but she left me to my own devices.

I was left with nothing but my wits and ready tongue.

I am selling insurance, I said.

What kind of insurance is it that is sold in pitch darkness, he asked.

It is only that I know your wife, I said.

My wife, he said, how do you know my wife?

I mean to say, I met your wife, I corrected.

And where exactly did you meet my wife, he asked.

I was here earlier selling insurance, and she said she could not make such an important decision without you being here, and so I thought I would come later.

In the end, it was the newspapers that I carried

under my arm that did it, it was *Kwayedza*, the local-language newspaper that always had an intoxicating mix of stories of witchcraft and adultery all delivered in the moralising tone that you associated with your oldest aunt. '*Kitsi Yakapfekedzwa Sekacheche*', said the headline of the day, 'Little Kitten Found Dressed as a Baby', and I could see my woman's man flicking his eyes towards it. I had a couple of other papers in the car, and I offered him these now, and also mentioned the two warm beers. This was all the oil that was needed to grease my way in. I had noticed before as I travelled to these remote parts of the country that the best way to a man's confidence was to offer anything printed, a book, a newspaper, a Watchtower pamphlet. I had made many friends by simply allowing someone, sometimes as many as six people, to read a newspaper over my shoulder. His eyes positively glinted at the wealth I presented him, for in addition to *Kwayedza*, I had in my car the *Daily Gazette*, *Parade* and *Horizon*.

We sat outside and read in the light glowing from the windows. I offered him an Everest, he took it and we smoked and drank our two warm beers in silence. Mabel, in the meantime, had disappeared to a kitchen from which enticing smells were coming. After half the *Kwayedza* and three cigarettes, I thought it sufficiently safe to mention my itinerancy and asked where I could spend the night.

Anything would be better than another night in the cramped confines of the Datsun, I said. I would not even mind sleeping on the floor, ha, ha, ha.

Hotel California Bed and Breakfast is just half a kilometre from here, he said. He gave me such detailed and concise directions that I could only take the hint, and thank him for his trouble. I said my goodbyes, and turned my car in the direction indicated.

I could not see much of the hotel in the dark, but it looked more like an overextended house than a hotel. The sound of the car attracted a man who came to the door to greet me. Welcome, welcome, he said in Shona. *Mauya, mauya ku*Hotel California.

This made me grin, of course, it reminded me of the Eagles song, and of the game that gave my brothers and me endless amusement as we translated the lyrics of English songs into Shona. And you know that once a song gets into your head, you can't get it out. The Eagles played in my head almost the entire time that I was there, and for a good many days afterwards.

In the light of what passed as the lobby, I was able to take a closer look at my host. He had in his mouth a matchstick which he had probably been using as a toothpick. It was stuck between two of his teeth, and moved up and down as he talked. You are a very lucky young man, he said. I am full up tonight, but just for you, I can create a vacancy.

He took my money for the one night, pointed me to the toilet at my request, and said I was just in time for a hot meal; it would be served in the sitting room. He then led me to a room where five men sat on two sets of matching sofas in a check-check pattern. They made room for me, and I found myself squashed between two of them. The only thing on the walls was a portrait of the President, only this was taken in the days he was the Prime Minister and had not yet started dyeing his hair. It hung at a slightly crooked angle above the television which was turned on to the news. Inflation had risen to eight point eighty-five per cent in the last quarter, said the news anchor, but the Finance Minister had urged the public not to panic because there was no danger at all of reaching double digits.

Every minute or so, someone would get up to adjust the aerial and the picture would clear before going fuzzy again. I had not been seated for ten minutes before a young woman entered with the food. I watched her, unsure as to which was more attractive to me at that moment, her firm breasts and bottom or the plates piled high with *sadza,* leaf vegetables and stewed pig trotters that she set down before us.

Now, I am not supposed to eat pork; my father's family is of the *mbeva* totem, and according to their wisdom, the humble mouse and pig are somehow related, and I am not supposed to touch the meat of either. But I was hungry and the trotters smelled inviting. It would not be the first time that I disobeyed my ancestors' edict, I reasoned to myself, and, promising a future libation, I laid aside my ancestors' scruples and tucked in. I had no idea that pig feet could taste so good. Perhaps it was my wilful disobedience of my ancestors that caused what happened later.

❧

By the time I had got to this point, my new friend had to slow down his car. POLICE AHEAD, said a sign. The good old boys in brown shorts and tunics, Harare's finest blackmailers, had set up a police roadblock next to the intersection just after the national sports stadium. The car stopped and a smiling policeman came up to the driver's window. He peered in and asked my new friend to switch on his indicator lights.

Everything was in order.

Wipers, he said.

They whirred silently.

The hooter, he said.

267

It gave a reassuring blare.

He beckoned over to two of his colleagues and nodded to them to stand behind the car.

Handbrake, he said.

The two policemen strained as they pushed the car from behind.

It did not budge.

Licence disc and driver's licence, the policeman said.

My young friend had both, and the disc was still valid.

*Tivhurireiwo ku*back, *vakuru*, was the next command, and my friend obeyed and opened the tailgate. There was nothing more sinister in the hatch than a spare tyre which the policeman took out with great ceremony. He bounced it up and down on the road as if testing it before returning it to its place.

He peered to see whether I had my seatbelt on.

It rested securely against my chest.

He then looked into the back of the car.

And why are these three passengers not secured, he asked.

What law says back passengers have to have seat belts, I said.

Is this your car, *vakuru*, the policeman asked me, and to the driver, he said, You will have to pay a spot fine of one million each for these three unsecured passengers. As my new friend joined me in protesting, the policeman told us that we could discuss it further at the police station if we wished.

Unfortunately, he added, the station is rather busy at this time, and you will not be attended to for at least five hours.

My friend opened his glove compartment, took out three million dollars and paid the fine.

I have no receipt books, the policeman said, You know how it is, so many shortages, what with all these international sanctions against the country. You will have to come to the police station next week to ask for it.

He must be relatively new at this, I thought. An old hand would not even have bothered to make these excuses. He waved us on our way, and, after we had each paid our share of the money for the fine to our driver, he and the others urged me to continue my story.

❧

After the meal was over, I asked the proprietor of the Hotel California if he had any beer. I was feeling generous after the meal, and thought I would treat my companions to a round or two.

We have only opaque beer, he said.

It was good enough, and soon we were all passing around a carton of Shake-Shake as we watched a football game that followed the news. The Hotel California began to take on a more pleasant aspect. We shared about six cartons in this manner, until, feeling tired, I asked for my bed. The matchstick man directed me to a bedroom. The blankets were not the fluffiest, nor were the sheets the cleanest; the whole looked like it had last seen soap and water in the days of Ian Smith, but I was too tired to care. I do not remember falling asleep, but I must have done so because I began to dream that there were sounds of moaning and laughter all around me. I suddenly woke up. It took a minute for me to remember where I was. I looked at my Sanyo, it was almost midnight. I remembered where I was. Then, through the walls came the sound of moans and laughter. It had not been a dream.

The moans came again.

Then laughter.

Moans.

Laughter.

There was a murmur of voices.

Then, Eh, eh, none of that funny stuff, said a woman's voice.

I will pay more, said a man's voice.

You do not have enough for that sort of thing, came back the response. The moans resumed. Despite myself, I was becoming aroused. The gentleman of the funny stuff was succeeded by a man, who, at the appropriate moment, shouted, *hau madoda*, *hau madoda* so loudly that I thought surely the entire hotel would hear him.

I found myself compelled to do what a man has to do when he finds himself in great need without a partner. But I was afraid of my host finding stains on his bedding. Besides, there was the unsavoury state of the bedding; I was pretty sure something would be fertilised. So I took out one of the condoms that I had hoped to use with Mabel, opened it and sheathed myself.

I no longer remember why I did this, but I also took off my clothes. I knelt on the bed and remembered the advice that my friend Robson had once given me; it is sometimes good, he had said, to use the left hand and rest the right – it will feel like you are cheating on yourself.

Indeed it did. I was about to do a *hau madoda*, *hau madoda* of my own when I heard the sound of footsteps leading to my room and the sound of my door opening. I dived under the blanket and pulled it up to my chin.

The door opened fully and in walked the proprietor of the Hotel California Bed and Breakfast. He switched on the light. I blinked and stared at him over the blanket.

You are still up, he said.

271

I nodded and smiled weakly and said nothing.

You said you were tired, he said.

Very tired, I said, and feigned a yawn.

I had a long day too, he said. It is probably because the days tend to be rather long at this time of year.

He stretched and yawned and talked on. It had been a dry year, he said. No rains at all this year. Would the rains ever come, he wondered. He did not know. No one knew for sure. Even the farming report could not be certain. Did I like Radio 2? He could not pass a day without listening to *Kwaziso*.

Even in my discomfort, I marvelled that the matchstick in his mouth still did not budge as he talked. A burst of laughter almost escaped from me but the urge to laugh soon ceased. With mounting horror, I watched as he took off all his clothes except for his underwear and got into bed beside me.

I was too startled to say anything. Under the blanket, I was naked but for the condom. I was suddenly aware of it – the smell of latex seemed to fill the room. I wondered that he did not notice it. I clutched the blanket closer. He reached for his share of it. I moved right to the edge of the bed, and lay there. He spoke. I pretended not to hear.

Meanwhile the sounds from next door continued, but I had ceased to care. I lay back until his breathing became even and I was sure that he was asleep. I eased my hold on the blanket, and as I did so, he shifted in my direction. I froze again. This continued for what seemed like half the night, until finally he began to snore, and I relaxed a little.

I must stay awake, I told myself, I must stay awake.

I woke up to find the sun in my face and my sleeping companion gone. I leaped out of bed and looked on my body for the condom. It was not there. I thought it might have got stuck to my back and craned and twisted my neck and felt for it, but to no avail. I shook the blankets and sheets. I shook my clothes. I shook the pillows. I even lifted the mattress and searched under the bed. I could only conclude that it must have slid off during the night and been picked up by my companion.

I put on my clothes, moved to the sitting room and tried to sneak out of the building to my car.

Good morning, said my bedfellow.

He spoke from a corner where he sat dunking bread and margarine into a mug of tea. His matchstick moved with his mouth. I had enough wits about me to wonder whether it was the same one from the day before.

Good morning, I said, I must be off.

What about breakfast, he said, we offer bed and breakfast.

I must press on, I said.

Drive well, he said.

He grinned and waved.

I ran to my car and drove out of Kamativi like I had all of Legion's demons after me.

~

By the time I had finished my story, my Prado friend and I had become firm friends. *Muri vahombe, m'dhara*, he said, You are really something. We dropped off the others and he insisted on buying me a drink. He even gave me back the million that I had paid him for the lift. I only got home well after seven that night – we ended up drinking first at Londoner's then at Tipperary's. He drove me home afterwards and we parted on the friendliest terms.

Shaky called me just as I was waving him off. I was in such fine spirits that I had almost forgotten the soured petrol deal.

Diamonds, *m'dhara*, Shaky said. I am with someone who knows someone who can get us into diamonds.

I walked into the house with the phone to my ear and listened as he talked about the diamonds that had been discovered in Marange and that would make us, him and me, rich beyond all our dreams.

❧ Acknowledgements ❧

The stories in this volume originally appeared as follows: 'At the Sound of the Last Post' in *African Pens: New Writing from Southern Africa* and in *Prospect*, under the title 'Oration for a Dead Hero'; 'An Elegy for Easterly' in *Jungfrau: Stories from the Caine Prize 2006*; 'Something Nice from London' and 'The Annexe Shuffle' in *Per Contra*; 'The Mupandawana Dancing Champion' and 'In the Heart of the Golden Triangle' in the Weaver Press anthologies *Laughing Now* and *Women Writing Zimbabwe*. I am grateful to my first editors at these publications, particularly Will Skidelsky and Miriam N. Kotzin who took a chance on an unknown writer and set me firmly on this path.

I also wish to thank everyone at Janklow & Nesbit (UK), and particularly Claire Paterson, agent extraordinaire, without whom none of this would have been possible, Rebecca Folland who successfully sold me to the world, Jenny McVeigh who brought me to Janklow and Eric Simonoff who made me want to stay.

At Faber, many thanks are due to my fantastic editors Mitzi Angel and Lee Brackstone for their good humour, their patience and their eagle eyes, and for loving these stories while making them better. Thank you to everyone involved with this book at both Faber and at Farrar, Straus and Giroux, especially Helen Francis, David Watkins, Chantal Clarke, Becky Fincham, Sarita Varma and Jeff Seroy. I also thank publisher Stephen Page for welcoming me so warmly to Faber.

Then there are the many friends who gave me rooms of my own and more, who rooted for me at every turn, who endured the I-want-to-be-a-writer lament for far longer than they deserved, and who are required to buy at least five books each now that I have mentioned them by name: Victoria Donaldson, Ben Mbengeranwa, Ingrid Cox-Lockhart, Martin Mbugua Kimani, Itai Madamombe, Sybilla Fries, Barbara and Gilbert Walter, Athita Komindr, Ian Donovan, Lisa Jacobs, Bonnie Galvin, Niall Meagher, Tom Sebastian, Hunter Nottage, Fernando Pierola, Pamela Collett, Chuma Nwokolo, Dirk Mueller-Ingrand, Nemdi and Olufemi Elias, Rob Campbell, Donata Rugarabamu, Bathsheba Okwenje, Marlon Zakeyo, Delice Gwaze, Ali Menzies, Maureen Chitewe, Jessie Majome, Thoko Moyo, Suzana Vukadinovic, Steve Thom, Luigi

Principi, Werner Zdouc, Lindy Nleya, Justin Fox, Molara Wood, Silvia Candido, Gugulethu Moyo, Muhtar Bakare, Binyavanga Wainaina, Shailja Patel, Munyaka Makuyana and Darrel Bristow-Bovey.

I also wish to thank Terence Ranger, Stephen Chan, Irene Staunton, Dolores and Anthony Fleischer and the South African Centre of International PEN, Helen and Nick Elam, Jamal Mahjoub, Veronique Tadjo, Susan Tiberghien, Eunice Scarfe and everyone at the Geneva Writers' Group, my many friends at the Zoetrope Virtual Studio, and my wonderful colleagues at the Advisory Centre on WTO Law, and in particular, Carol Lau, Leo Palma and Frieder Roessler. Finally, I wish to thank Jane Hirshfield and Oliver Mtukudzi for allowing me to use their words, J. M. Coetzee for his generosity and Silas Chekera for everything.